William Burdon

Every Man His Own Farrier

Containing Ten Minutes' Advice how to buy a horse - to which is added

directions on how to use your horse at home or on a Journey

William Burdon

Every Man His Own Farrier
Containing Ten Minutes' Advice how to buy a horse - to which is added directions on how to use your horse at home or on a Journey

ISBN/EAN: 9783337127763

Printed in Europe, USA, Canada, Australia, Japan

Cover: Foto ©Andreas Hilbeck / pixelio.de

More available books at **www.hansebooks.com**

EVERY MAN HIS OWN FARRIER.

CONTAINING

TEN MINUTES' ADVICE

HOW TO BUY A HORSE.

TO WHICH IS ADDED

DIRECTIONS HOW TO USE YOUR HORSE AT HOME OR ON A JOURNEY; AND WHAT REMEDIES ARE PROPER FOR ALL THE DISEASES TO WHICH HE IS LIABLE.

PHILADELPHIA:

LEARY, GETZ & CO.

224 NORTH SECOND STREET.

1860.

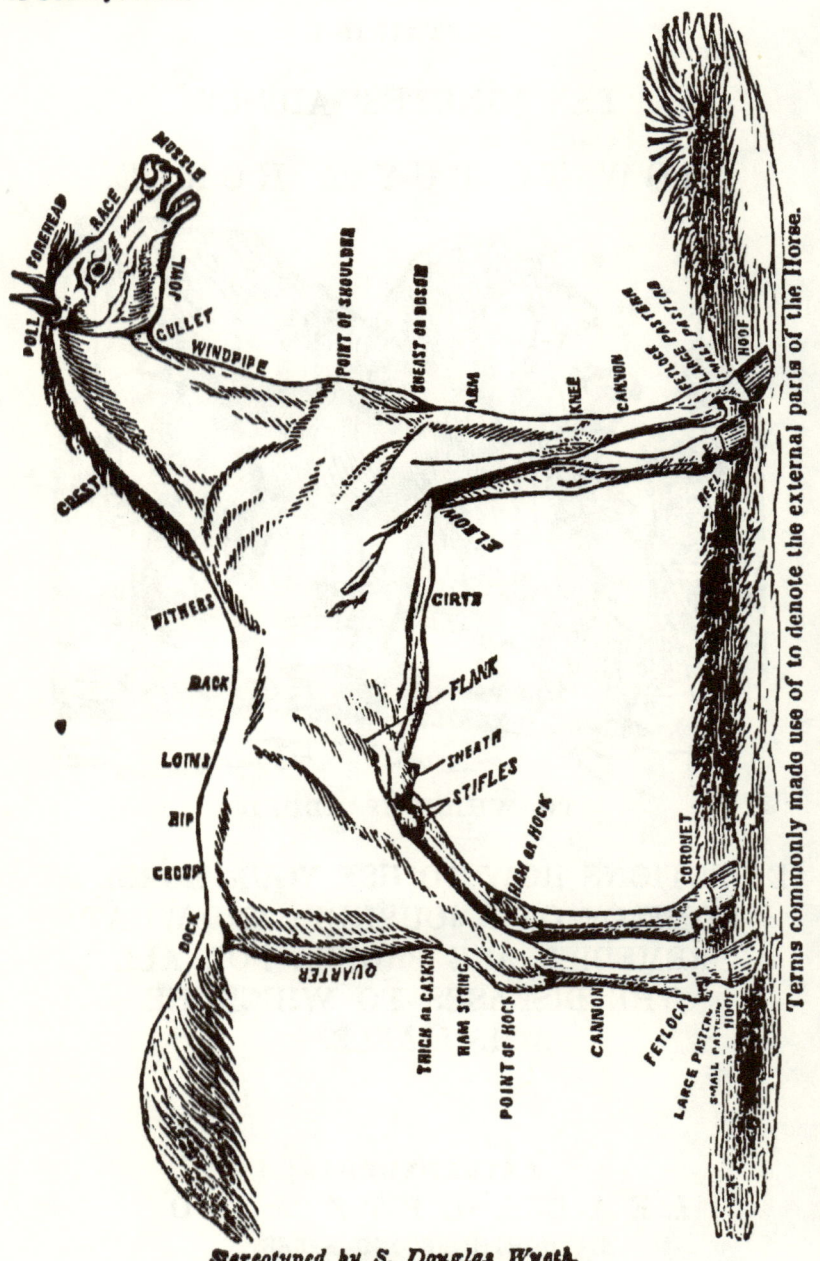

Stereotyped by S. Douglas Wyeth, No. 7 Pear St., Philadelphia.

CONTENTS

OF

"TEN MINUTES' ADVICE."

CONTENTS

OF

"DIRECTIONS HOW TO USE A HORSE ON A JOURNEY."

CONTENTS.

INTRODUCTION.

The following short treatise was compiled with intent to guard the unwary from deceptions in the purchase of a Horse, as well as to refresh the memory of gentlemen better acquainted with the requisite qualifications of that noble animal.

The remarks are drawn from long, and, in some instances, dear-bought experience, in the snares which jockies and grooms in general lay before those who are under the necessity of dealing with them.

The author therefore presumes to hope, that the attempt is praiseworthy, and if in any instance he is found mistaken, the favour of any further hint, for the improvement of a future edition, addressed to the publisher, will be most thankfully received, and properly attended to.

Having premised thus much, it is proper that we should introductorily remark,

That a large shin-bone, that is, long from the knee to the pastern, in a foal, shows a tall horse.

Double the space in a foal, new foaled, betwixt the knee and withers, will, in general, be the height of him when a complete horse.

Foals that are of stirring spirits, wanton of disposition, active in leaping, running and chasing, ever leading the way, and striving for mastery, always prove horses of excellent mettle; and those of the contrary disposition, most commonly jades.

Before we enter on any particular observations, it may not be unnecessary to give one general rule, which experience has proved to be a good one, that is—*No Foot, No Horse.*

A horse's ability, and continuance in goodness, is known by his hoofs. If they are strong, smooth, hard, deep, tough, upright, and hollow, that horse cannot be a very bad one; for they are the foundation of his building, and give a fortitude to all the rest; and if otherwise, he cannot be remarkably good or lasting.

Without further preface, we refer the reader to the particular remarks and observations contained in the " Ten Minutes' Advice."

TO THE READER.

Annexed to the " Ten Minutes' Advice," will be found a complete " Pocket Farrier," containing a series of Directions how to use a Horse on a Journey, with receipts and cures for the different diseases to which he is liable.

It may not be unnecessary to acquaint the reader, that these prescriptions have not been hastily jumbled together, but are experimentally efficacious; and, small as this tract may appear, it will be found to inform gentlemen,

I. What methods are best to be used if their horses fall lame.

II. What medicines are proper to give them, when sick, and

III. How to direct the operations, and escape the impositions of ignorant men.

In short, by the help of this treatise, gentlemen will be able to prevent a groom or farrier from injuring their horses, by improper applications, and mistaking one distemper for another.

It points out the best remedies at first, and the reader may be assured they have been experimentally confirmed by a practice of thirty years. The book is drawn up in a manner calculated for a gentleman's pocket, supposing him upon a journey; and no man who values his horse, should presume to travel without it.

TEN MINUTES' ADVICE

HOW TO BUY A HORSE.

IT is a common observation that in the art of horse-manship, by far the most difficult part is that of giving proper directions for purchasing a horse free from fault and blemish. The deceptions in this branch of traffic being looked on in a less fraudulent light than they seem to deserve, and of consequence are more frequently practised, it shall therefore be our business, in the follow-ing brief remarks, to show, in the best manner we are able, the imperfections which, from either nature or mis-chance, every horse is liable to.

IN THE STABLE.

See the horse you are about to purchase, in the stable, and without any person being in the stall with him, and if he has any complaint in his legs he will soon show it, by altering the situation of them, taking up one and set-ting down the other; and this denotes his being foundered or over-worked.

On ordering him out, let no one be the last in the stable but yourself; you should also, if possible, be the

7

first in, lest the owner, or some of his quick emissaries, take an opportunity to fig him; a practice common among dealers, in order to make the tail show as if carried very high, when, in reality, the day after, he will, in appearance, be five pounds worse.

THE EYES.

This is the proper time to examine his eyes, which may be done in a dark stable, with a candle, or rather in the day time when he is led from the stall; cause the man who leads him to stop at the stable door just as his head peeps out, and all his body still within. If the white of the eye appears reddish at the bottom, or of a colour like a withered leaf, I would not advise you to purchase him. A moon-eyed horse is known by his weeping, and keeping his eyes almost shut at the beginning of the distemper: as the moon changes, he gradually recovers his sight, and in a fortnight or three weeks sees as well as before he had the disorder. Dealers, when they have such a horse to sell, at the time of his weeping always tell you that he has got a bit of straw or hay in his eye, or that he has received some blow: they also take care to wipe away the humour, to prevent its being seen; but a man should trust only himself in buying of horses, and above all, be very exact in examining the eyes. In this he must have regard to time and place where he makes the examination. Bad eyes may appear good in winter, when snow is upon the ground; and often, good ones appear bad according to the position of the horse. Never examine a horse's eyes by the side of a white wall, where the dealers always choose to show one that is moon-eyed..

The moon-eyed horse has always one eye bigger than the other, and above his lids you may generally discover wrinkles or circles.

If you observe a fleshy excrescence that proceeds from the corner of the eye, and covers a part of the pupil, and is in shape almost like the beard of an oyster, though seemingly a matter of no great consequence, yet it is what I call a whitlow in the eye, and if suffered to grow, it draws away a part of the nourishment of the eye, and sometimes occasions a total privation of sight: on the contrary, if the eyes are round, big, black and shining; if the black of the eye fill the pit, or outward circumference, so that in moving, very little of the white appears, they are signs of goodness and mettle. Large eyes are in general esteemed the best, but be sure to observe that the chrystaline be thoroughly transparent, for without that, no kind of eye can be said to be good.

The eye that is of a long oval figure is almost always weak, especially if the corners are narrow for a considerable way.

We may here observe that no animal is so subject to blindness as the horse. This arises from the great heat of his blood, and the constant feverish state in which his great exertions keep him, which occasions inflammation, and thickening of the extremely thin membrane that covers the eye.

Most people, in examining a horse's eyes, lead him under a shed and look sideways through the eye towards the light, to ascertain whether it be clear and transparent as it ought; but the best way is to make the observation when he first comes out of a dark stable into strong daylight; for if he has any weakness in his eyes, he will contract or wrinkle his brow and look upward to receive more light; and if, at the same time, the

pupil of the eye appears large, or does not contract, it is
a bad sign; for that reason it is best to observe a horse's
eyes first in the shade, taking notice of the dimensions of
the pupil, for if that lessens on his coming into a stronger
light it is a sure sign that his sight is good and likely to
continue so.

Upon the whole, that eye is generally good where
the eyelids are thin, the eye transparent and sprightly,
and when the horse has a bold resolute look, and takes
notice of the different objects that present themselves
before him without fear.

One of the best signs of a good horse is the eyes
wide apart.

COUNTENANCE.

After having carefully satisfied yourself as to his
eyes, let him be brought out, and have him stand naked
before you; then take a strict view of his countenance,
particularly with regard to the cheerfulness of it, this
being an excellent glass to observe his goodness and best
perfections. Be careful you are not deceived by the
marks in his face, as frequently a good-looking star is
made of cat's skin. If his ears be small, sharp, short,
pricked, and moving; or if they are long, but yet well
set on, and well carried, it is a mark of goodness; if
they are thick, laved, or lolling, wide set, and unmoving,
they are signs of dulness, and of an evil nature.

The whole substance of the ears should be thin and
delicate. They ought to be placed on the very top of
the head, and their extremities or points when pricked
up should be nearer than their roots. When a horse
carries his ears pointed forwards he is said to have a
bold, hardy, or brisk ear; and it is a perfection in a

horse's ears when he is travelling to have them firm, and not mark every motion of his feet by a slouch of his ears like a hog.

A lean forehead, swelling outward, the mark or feather in his face set high, with a white star or ratch of an indifferent size, and even placed, or a white snip on the nose or lip, they are all marks of beauty and goodness; on the contrary, a fat, cloudy, or frowning countenance, the mark in his face standing low, as under his eyes, if his star or ratch stand awry, and instead of a snip, his nose be raw, and unhairy, or his face generally bald, they are signs of deformity.

THE STRANGLES.

This is a distemper to which colts and young horses are particularly liable. It begins with a swelling between the jaw-bones, which frequently extends to the muscles of the tongue, and is generally attended with great heat, pain, and inflammation.

In purchasing a horse, handle his cheeks or chaps, and if you find the bones lean and thin, the space wide between them, the thropple or wind-pipe big as you can gripe, and the void place without knots or kernels, and the jaws so great that the neck seems to couch within them, they are all signs of great wind, courage, soundness of head and body ; on the contrary, if the chaps are fat and thick, the space between them closed up with gross substance, and the thropple little, they are signs of short wind and much inward foulness: should the void place be full of knots and kernels, beware of the strangles or glanders, the former of which may be easily discovered by the swelling between the two nether jaw-bones, which discharges a white matter. There is also a disorder which is called the Bastard Strangles, which appears sometimes like, and sometimes different from the true strangles. The bastard strangles are what proves the horse has not thrown off his true strangles, but that some foul humours are still left behind; this disorder may come at four, five, six, or even seven years of age. A continual languor at work, and seemingly perpetually weary, without any visible ailment, is a certain sign that he is not clear of this disorder, which sometimes will affect the foot, the leg, the ham, the haunch, the shoulder, the breast, or the eye, and without care in this latter case, may corrupt the pupil of the eye, as the small-pox does in men.

MORE FOUNDERING.

There is also another disorder, much like the strangles, which is called Morefoundering, (the word is of French origin) and is used by farriers to distinguish those colds which a horse takes by being suffered to cool too suddenly after violent exercise—and may be known by a running at the nose.

GLANDERS.

A distemper in horses which too generally proves fatal, notwithstanding the many boasted remedies that are prescribed for its cure. In fact all horses that are said to die of the glanders, are victims to a pulmonary consumption, the lungs of all such being found diseased or destroyed.

This disease is known by a flux or running of corrupt matter from the nostrils, which is of different colours, according as the disease is more or less inveterate, white, yellow, green, and sometimes almost black, and very fœtid, in which case it may be concluded that the bones are become foul.

In buying a horse, feel if he has any flat glands fastened to the nether jaw, which give him pain when you press them, and remember that a running at one nostril is worse than at both.

VIVES.

When the jaws are strait, that the neck swells above them, it is a sign of short wind; but if the swelling be long, and close by his chaps, like a whetstone, then be sure he has the vives, which only differs from the strangles in this, that the swellings of the kernels under the ears seldom gather or come to matter.

When these swellings appear in an old or full aged horse, they are signs of great malignity, and often of an inward decay, as well as forerunners of the glanders.

This is a distemper most frequent in high mountainous countries, especially to horses that are not used to the crudities produced in the stomach by the spring and fountain waters that rise in hilly grounds. Standing waters or those of very little current, are the least dangerous, and seldom cause the vives, but very deep wells arc bad.

NOSTRILS.

If his nostrils be open, dry, wide, and large, so as upon any straining the inward redness is discovered, if his muzzle be small, his mouth deep, and his lips equally meeting, they are signs of health and wind; but should

2

his nostrils be strait, his wind is then little. Should you find the muzzle to be gross, his spirit will be dull. Nothing contributes more to a horse's breathing easy, and with freedom, than the wideness of his nostrils.

THE MOUTH.

If a horse's mouth be shallow he will never carry the bitt well, and if his upper will not reach his under lip, old age and infirmity mark him for carrion. When the mouth is cloven too much, there is a good deal of difficulty to bitt a horse so that he may not " swallow it," as horsemen term it. The compliance and obedience of a horse in the manége, is owing, in a great measure, to the tender, or quick sense of his mouth, which renders him fearful of being hurt by the bitt. A horse that has a very fine mouth will stop if his rider merely bends his body backward and raise his hand, without waiting for the check of the bridle.

AGE.

Respecting the age of a horse that is fit for work, he should have forty teeth; twenty-four grinders, which teach us nothing, and sixteen others, which have their names, and discover his age. As mares usually have no tusks, their teeth are only thirty-six. A colt is foaled without teeth; in a few days he puts out four which are called pincers, or nippers; soon after appear the four separators : Next to the pincers, it is sometimes three or four months before the next, called corner teeth, push forth. These twelve colt's teeth, in the front of the mouth, continue, without alteration, till the colt is two years, or two years and a half old, which makes it difficult, without great care, to avoid being imposed on during the interval, if the seller finds it his interest to make the colt pass for either younger or older than he really is; the only rule you have then to judge by is his coat, and the hairs of his mane and tail. A colt of one year has a supple, rough coat, resembling that of a water spaniel, and the hair of his mane and tail feels like flax, and hangs like a rope untwisted; whereas a colt of two years has a flat coat, and straight hairs, like a grown horse.

At about two years and a half old, sometimes sooner, sometimes later, according as he has been fed, a horse begins to change his teeth. The pincers, which come the first, are also the first that fall; so that at three years he has four horse's, and eight colt's teeth, which are easily known apart, the former being larger, flatter, and yellower than the other, and streaked from the end quite into the gums.

These four horse pincers have, in the middle of their extremities, a black hole, very deep; whereas those of the colt are round and white. When the horse is coming four years old, he loses his four separators, or middle teeth, and puts forth four others, which follow the same rule as the pincers. He has now eight horse's teeth, and four colt's. At five years old he sheds the four corner, which are his last colt's teeth, and is called a horse.

During this year also, his four tusks (which are chiefly peculiar to horses) come behind the others; the lower ones often four months before the upper; but whatever may be vulgarly thought, a horse that has the two lower tusks, if he has not the upper, may be judged to be under five years old, unless the other teeth show the contrary; for some horses that live to be very old

never have any upper tusks at all. The two lower tusks
are one of the most certain rules that a horse is coming
five years old, notwithstanding his colt's teeth may not
be all gone.

Jockies and breeders, in order to make their colts
seem five years old when they are but four, pull out
their last colt's teeth; but if all the colt's teeth are gone,
and no tusks appear, you may be certain this trick has
been played. Another artifice they use, is to beat the
bars every day with a wooden mallet, in the place where
the tusks are to appear, in order to make them seem
hard, as if the tusks were just ready to cut.

When a horse is coming six years old, the two lower
pincers fill up, and, instead of the holes above-mentioned,
show only a black spot. Between six and seven the two
middle teeth fill up in the same manner; and between
seven and eight the corner teeth do the like; after which
it is said to be impossible to know certainly the age of
a horse, he having no longer any mark in the mouth.

You can indeed only have recourse to the tusks, and
the situation of the teeth, of which I shall now speak.

For the tusks you must with your finger feel the
inside of them from the point quite to the gum. If the
tusk be pointed flat, and has two little channels within
side, you may be certain the horse is not old, and at the
utmost only coming ten. Between eleven and twelve
the two channels are reduced to one, which after twelve
is quite gone, and the tusks are as round within as they
are without; you have no guide then but the situation
of the teeth. The longest teeth are not always a sign
of the greatest age, but their hanging over and pushing
forward, as their meeting, perpendicularly, is a certain
token of youth.

Many persons, whilst they see certain little holes in
the middle of the teeth, imagine, that such horses are

but in their seventh year, without regard to the situation the teeth take as they grow old.

When horses are young, their teeth meet perpendicularly, but grow longer, and push forward with age: besides, the mouth of a young horse is very fleshy within in the palate, and his lips are firm and hard : on the contrary, the inside of an old horse's mouth is lean both above and below, and seems to have only the skin upon the bones. The lips are soft and easy to turn up with the hand.

All horses are marked in the same manner, but some naturally, and others artificially. The natural mark is called Begue, and some ignorant persons imagine such horses are marked all their lives, because for many years they find a little hole, or a kind of void in the middle of the separators and corner teeth ; but when the tusks are grown round, as well within as without, and the teeth point forward, there is room to conjecture in proportion as they advance from year to year, what the horse's age may be, without regarding the cavity above mentioned.

The artificial manner is made use of by dealers and jockies, who mark their horses, after the age of them is known, to make them appear only six or seven years old. They do it in this manner : They throw down the horse to have him more at command, and, with a steel graver, like what is used for ivory, hollow the middle teeth a little, and the corner ones somewhat more ; then fill the holes with a little rosin, pitch, sulphur, or some grains of wheat, which they burn in with a bit of hot wire, made in proportion to the hole. This operation they repeat from time to time, till they give the hole a lasting black, in imitation of nature ; but in spite of all they can do, the hot iron makes a little yellowish circle round these holes, like what it would leave upon ivory ; they have therefore another trick to prevent detection,

2 *

which is to make the horse foam from time to time, after having rubbed his mouth, lips, and gums with salt, and the crumb of bread dried and powdered with salt. This foam hides the circle made by the iron.

Another thing they cannot do, is, to counterfeit young tusks, it being out of their power to make those two crannies above mentioned, which are given by nature. With files they may make them sharper or flatter, but then they take away the shining natural enamel, so that one may always know, by these tusks, horses that are past seven, till they come to twelve or thirteen.

[FROM THE AMERICAN FARMER.]

AGE BY FEELING.

A wonderful discovery recently made in an old Horse's age!!

Since the age of that noble animal, the horse, after a certain period of life, (that is to say) after the marks in his *incisors* and *cuspidati* are entirely obliterated, to be able to ascertain his age, with any tolerable degree of certainty, appears to the generality of *" horse age judges,"* to be a subject of very much uncertainty, I now take the liberty of laying before the public, through the medium of your paper, an infallible method (subject to very few exceptions) of ascertaining it in such a manner, after a horse loses his marks, or after he arrives to the age of nine years or over ; so that any person concerned in horses, even of the meanest capacity, may not be imposed upon in a horse's age, from nine years of age and over, more than three years at farthest, until the animal arrives at the age of twenty years and upwards, *by just feeling the submaxillary bone, or the bone of the lower jaw.*

This method I discovered, by making many anatomical observations on the skulls of dead horses and repeated dissections. In order, therefore, to elucidate the above, I must in the first place beg leave to remark ; that the submaxillary bone, or the lower jaw bone of all young horses, about four or five years of age, immediately above the *bifurcation,* is invariably thick and very round at the bottom ; the cavity of said bone being very small, contains a good deal of marrow, and generally continues in this state until the animal arrives at that period which is generally termed an " aged horse," or until the animal acquires his full size in height or thickness ; or *according to sporting language, is completely furnished,* with very little variation. But after this period, the cavity as aforesaid becomes larger, and more marrow is contained therein. Hence the submaxillary bone becomes thinner and sharper a little above the *bifurcation.*

This indelible mark may always be observed in a small degree in horses above eight years of age ; but at nine years old it is still more perceptible. It continues growing a little thinner and sharper at the bottom until twelve years of age. From thence until fifteen, it is still thinner, and about as sharp as the back of a case knife near the handle. From this period until the ages 18, 19, 20, and upwards, it is exceedingly so ; and is as sharp, in many subjects, as the dull edge of that instrument.

RULES.

1st. Put your three fingers about half an inch or an inch immediately above the bifurcation, and grasp the submaxillary bone, or the lower jaw bone. If it is thick at the sides, and very round indeed at the bottom, the animal is most certainly under nine years of age.

2d. If the bone is not very thick, and it is perceivably not very round at the bottom, he is from nine to twelve years old, and so on. From twelve to fifteen, the bone is sharper at bottom, and thinner at the sides, the bottom is generally as sharp as the back of a case knife; and from 15 to 18, 19, 20, and upwards, without many exceptions, the bone, when divested of its integuments, is as sharp as the dull edge of that instrument.

3d. Allowances must always be made between heavy, large western or wagon horses, or carriage horses, and fine blooded ones. By practising and strictly attending to the above rules, upon all descriptions of horses, the performer in a little time will become very accurate in the accomplishment of his desires, more especially if he attentively observes the lower jaw bone of dead horses."

THE BARBS, THE LAMPAS, GIGGS UPON THE LIPS, AND GAGG-TEETH.

As the defects of the mouth may destroy a horse without any distemper, it will here be proper to give information as follows:

For the *barbs*, look under the horse's tongue, and see if he has not two fleshy excrescences on the under palate, like little bladders. It seems to be a mere trifle, but these, however, will hinder a horse from drinking as usual; and if he does not drink freely, he eats the less, and languishes from day to day, perhaps, without any one's taking notice of it.

The *lampas* is known by opening the horse's mouth, and looking at his upper palate, to see if the flesh comes down below the inner teeth: this gives him pain in eating his oats, and even his hay, when it is too harsh; though he can very well manage bran, grass, or kind hay. The lampas causes a horse to look rueful and fall away.

When you have looked into the horse's mouth, without finding either the lampas or the barbs, turn up his lips both upper and under, and perhaps you may find what are termed *giggs*, consisting of small swellings or pustules on the inside of the lips, which will sometimes increase to the size of a large walnut, at which advanced state they are so painful that the horse will let his meat fall out of his mouth, or keep it there unchewed, sooner than attempt to eat it. This defect may be felt with the finger, and is what hinders horses from eating as usual; and this is what is called giggs upon the lips.

Gagg-teeth does not often happen to young horses, though sometimes it is met with; and is to be discovered by putting the colt's-foot into the mouth, and looking at the large grinders, which in this case appear unequal, and in eating catch hold of the inside of the cheeks, causing great pain and making them refuse their food.

THE BREAST.

The breast of a horse should be full and large, and you should look from his head down to his breast, and see that it be broad, outswelling, and adorned with many features, for this shows strength: the little, or small breast shows weakness, as the narrow one is apt to stumble.

THE ANTICOR, OR ANTICOW.

This is a malignant swelling in the throat and breast

of a horse, extending in some cases to the very sheath under the belly, and is mortal to horses if they are not soon relieved.

In going to purchase, put your hand between his fore-legs, and you can very readily feel if he has or has not such a swelling. Anticor proceeds from different causes, viz. the remains of an old distemper which was never perfectly cured, or after which the horse was too soon put to labour; from too much heat contracted in the stable, by being kept up a long time without airing, or from having lost too large a quantity of blood in what part soever the vein was opened. When you touch a swelling of this kind, the impressions of the fingers remain for some time, as if you had made them in a bit of puff paste, filling up again by degrees as the paste would rise. This swelling contains bloody water, that insinuates between the flesh and the skin, and proves that all the blood in the veins is corrupted.

THE THIGHS AND LEGS.

See that the fore-thighs be rush grown, well horned within, sinewed, fleshy and outswelling; those being signs of strength, as the contrary are of weakness. If his knees bear a proportion to each other, be lean, sinewy, and close knit, they are good; but if one is bigger or rounder than the other, the horse has received mischief; if they are gross, he is gouty, and if he has scars, or the hair be broken, beware of a stumbling jade, and perpetual faller.

The hind parts, from the hip-bone to the hock, should be of great length; the hind legs should be full of sinew, clear of knots, and rather crooked than straight in the hock. Be careful to avoid buying a horse knock-kneed.

or with feet turned in or out, for a horse of this make never can be sure footed, and he moves ugly.

SPLINTS.

This may be looked upon as a disorder of the fore-legs, though occurring on the hind ones at times.

Look down his legs to his pasterns, and if you find them clean, lean, flat, sinewy, and the inward bought of his knee without seams, or hair broken, it shows a good shape and soundness; but if on the inside of the leg you find hard knots, they are splints, of which there are three sorts. The simple splint, which appears with-in the leg under the knee, remote from the great nerve and the joint of the knee, ought not to hinder a man from buying a good horse, for it gives him no pain, is only disagreeable to the sight, and goes away in time of itself. All the three sorts of splints are known by the same rule; for whenever you see a tumour upon the flat of the leg, whether within or without, if it be under the knee, and appears hard to the touch, it is a splint; and when it is situated as above described, it signifies no-thing; but when it comes upon the joint of the knee, without any interval, it loses the name of splint, and may be called a fusee; it then, as one may easily con-ceive, makes the leg of a horse stiff, and hinders him from bending his knee; consequently it obliges him to stumble, and even fall, and after a violent exercise makes him lame. Rest alone cures the lameness, but not the fusee.

The third kind of splint, whether within or without, is when you feel it between the nerve and the bone, and sometimes even at the end of the nerve; this is called a nervous splint, and is the worst of all the kinds; besides that, the horse is never here so firm footed, but that he limps at every little degree of labour.

OSSLETS.

There are also three kinds of osslets, which are of the same nature as splints, and some persons take them for the same thing; but there is this difference however between them, that splints come near the knees, and osslets near the fetlocks. Their seat is indifferently within or without the leg.

The first is the simple osslet, which does not grow near the joint of the fetlock or the nerve.

This need not hinder any man from buying a horse, because it puts him to no inconvenience, and very often goes away of itself without a remedy. The second is that which descends into the fetlock, and hinders the motion of that joint; this occasions a horse to stumble and fall, and with a very little work to become lame. The third has its seat between the bone and the nerve, and sometimes upon the nerve; it so much incommodes a horse, that he cannot stand firm, but limps on every little occasion.

WINDGALLS.

There are also three kinds of windgalls, which appear to the eye much like osslets, but are not, however, just in the same places; nor do they feel like them, for osslets are hard, but windgalls give way to the touch. Some horses are more liable to these than others, and that for several reasons. Some proceed from old worn-out sires, and others by being worked too young. A simple windgall is a little tumour, between the skin and the flesh, round the fetlocks: when it appears at a good distance from the large nerve, it does not lame the horse; and if he has but age on his side, that is, be under ten years old, at most, he will be as useful as before, provided the work you put him to, be not of the most laborious kind; however, a horse is much better without, than with even this sort of simple windgall, which consists of thin skins, full of red liquid, and soft to the touch. The nervous windgall answers the same description, only, as the simple ones come upon the fetlock, or a little above it, upon the leg bone, in the very place of osslets, nervous ones come behind the fetlock, upon the great nerve, which makes them of worse consequence, for they never fail to lame a horse after much fatigue. These windgalls may happen upon any of the legs, but some of them are more dangerous than others, in proportion as they press the nerve, and are capable of laming the horse; and take notice by the way, that windgalls are more troublesome in summer than in winter, especially in very hot weather, when the pores are all open. The third sort is the bloated windgall, and is of the worst sort when they come over the hind part of the fetlock, between the bone and the large nerve, and make the horse so lame at every little thing he does, that he can scarce set his foot on the ground: they appear on both sides the leg, without as well as within; and when you touch them with your hand or finger, they feel like a pig's or cow's bladder full of wind. If under his knees there are scabs on the inside, it is the speedy or swift cut, and in that case he will but ill endure galloping; if above the pasterns, on the inside, you find scabs, it shows interfering; but if the scabs be generally over his legs, it is either occasioned by foul keeping, or a spice of the mange.

It is seldom that a horse is found entirely clear of

3

windgalls, particularly about the hind legs, if he be much used.

THE PASTERN AND PASTERN-JOINT.

Take care that the pastern-joint be clear and well knit together, and that the pastern be strong, short and upright; for if the pastern-joint be big or swelled, beware of sinew strains; if the pastern be long, weak or bending, the limbs will hardly be able to carry the body without tiring. Indeed the experience of every one will tell you that horses with long pasterns cannot travel near so well as those with short ones.

HOOFS.

The hoofs should be proportioned to the size of the horse, black, smooth, tough, nearly round, deep, hollow, and full-sounding; for white hoofs are tender, and carry a shoe ill, and a brittle hoof will carry no shoe at all: a flat hoof, that is pumiced, shows foundering; and a hoof that is empty, and hollow-sounding, shows a decayed inward part, by reason of some wound or dry founder. If the hair lie smooth, and close about the crown of the hoof, and the flesh flat and even, then all is perfect; but should the hair be there rough, the skin scabbed, and the flesh rising, you may then be apprehensive of a ring bone, a crown scab, or a quittor bone.

Some horses' hoofs are not round, but broad, spreading out of the sides and quarters; such have, for the most part, narrow heels, and will at length come to be flat-hoofed, neither will they carry their shoes long, nor travel far, being apt to surbate or founder. Horses with crooked hoofs are splay-footed, and consequently go with their joints so close together, that they cannot travel without cutting or interfering, or, what is still worse, without striking one leg so hard against the other as to produce lameness.

CIRCLED FEET.

Circled feet are very easy to be known: they are, when you see little excrescences round the hoof, which enclose the foot, and appear like so many small circles. Dealers who have such horses, never fail to rasp round their hoofs, in order to make them smooth ; and to conceal the rasping, when they are to show them for sale, they black the hoofs all over ; for without that, one may easily perceive what has been done, and seeing the mark of the rasp, is a proof that the horse is subject to this accident. As to the causes, it proceeds from the remains of an old distemper, or from having been foundered ; and the disease being cured without care being taken of the feet, whereupon the circulation of the blood not being regularly made, especially round the crown, between the hair and the horn, the part loses its nourishment, and contracts or enlarges itself in proportion as the horse is worked. If these circles were only on the surface, the jockies' method of rasping them down would then be good for nothing; but they form themselves also within the feet, as well as without, and consequently press on the sensible part, and make a horse limp with ever so little labour. One may justly compare a horse in this situation, to a man that has corns on his feet, and yet is obliged to walk a long way in shoes that are too tight and stubborn : a horse therefore is worth a great deal less on this account.

BOW LEGGED.

After having well examined the feet, stand about three paces from his shoulders, and look carefully that he is not bow legged, which proceeds from two different causes; first, from nature, when a horse has been got by a worn out stallion; and secondly, from his having been worked too young; neither in the one case nor the other is the horse of any value, because he never can be sure-footed; it is also a disagreeable sight if the knees point forwards, and his legs turn in under him, so that the knees come much further out than the feet; it is what is called a bow legged horse, and such a one ought to be rejected for any service whatsoever, as he never can stand firm on his legs; and how handsome soever he may otherwise be, he should on no account be used for a stallion, because all his progeny will have the same deformity.

THE HEAD.

Stand by the horse's side and take particular notice that his head be well set on; for if thick set, be assured it will cause him to toss up his nose for want of wind, which causes a horse to carry his head disagreeably high, and occasions a ticklish mouth.   •

His face should be rather of the Roman order than straight.

The head of a horse should be narrow, lean, and not too long.

THE NECK AND THE MANE.

The neck of a horse is a part that adds greatly to his beauty or deformity.   •

His neck should be small at the setting on of his head, and long, growing deeper to the shoulders, with a high, strong, and thin mane, long, soft, and somewhat curling. The upper edge should form the half of an arch, gradually falling in height and shape from the head to the shoulders. A well-shaped neck contributes greatly to the horse's going light on the hand, as a coarse ill-shaped one does to making him go heavy.

Much hair on the mane shows dulness, as too thin a mane shows fury; and to have none, or if it be shed, is a proof of the worm in it, the itch, or manginess. The mane should be moderately thin, and in length half the width of the neck.

To have a short thick neck, like a bull, to have it falling on the withers, shows want of strength and mettle.

THE POLL-EVIL.

This is a large bigness or swelling in the nape of the neck, and the gentleman going to purchase can easily see by the size of the horse's neck whether he has it or not. It proceeds from some blow, bruise or external injury, and its consequences are much to be dreaded. John Hinds, a distinguished English farrier says, "the most prolific cause of poll-evil I am inclined to attribute to the low stable door-way, whereby the animal gets many a trivial hit at going in and coming out."

THE SHOULDERS.

The shoulders of a horse should be sharp and narrow at the withers, and thrown far back, for experience has proved that such as have low shoulders with high rumps,

3*

never show to advantage, and seldom make good saddle or race horses.*

In showing a horse, a dealer, or jockey, will generally place him with his fore feet on a higher ground than his hind ones, in order that the shoulder may appear further in his back, and make him higher in sight than he really is; but be sure to cause him to be led on level ground, and see that his shoulders lie well into his back; for an upright shouldered horse carries his weight too forward, which is disagreeable, and unsafe to the rider. Have his fore legs stand even, and you will then have it in your power to judge of his shoulders. If you do not observe this, the dealer will contrive that his near leg stands before the other, as the shoulders, in that position, appear to lay further in the back. If his knees stand nearly close, and his toes quite in a line, not turning in, nor yet turning out, be assured he will not cut; if he takes his legs up a moderate height, and neither clambers, nor yet goes too near the ground, he will most likely answer your purpose.

BACK, BODY, &c.

Observe that the chine of his back be broad, even and straight, his ribs well compassed, and bending outward, his fillets upright, strong, short, and above an handful between his last rib and his huckle bone; his belly should be well let down, yet hidden within his ribs, and his stones close thrust up to his body, those being marks of health and goodness. Be careful in observing that he has no swelling in his testicles, a disorder that

* Eclipse is the only instance, we believe, on record to the contrary. "The shoulder of Eclipse was a low one."

usually proceeds either from some strain in working, or from the horse's having continued too long in the stable, or from his putting one leg over any bar, and being checked by the halter, or, in a word, from any other accident that confines a horse, makes him kick or fling, and bruise his cods, and there is no other way of knowing this distemper, but by some outward swelling upon the part.

The coming down of the testicles proceeds from the same causes, with this difference only, that it is a long time of discovering itself; whereas the other may come in one night. If his chine be narrow, he will never carry a saddle well; and to have it bending or saddle backed, shows weakness. If his ribs be flat, there is but small liberty for wind. Should his fillets hang low, or weak, he will never climb a hill, or carry a burden well. A belly that is clung up, or gaunt, and stones hanging down loose, are signs of sickness, tenderness, foundering in the body, and unaptness for labour. His buttocks should be round, plump, full, and in an even level with his body: the narrow, pin buttock, the hog or swine rump, and the falling and down-let buttock, shows an injury in nature. The horse that is deep in his girthing place, is generally of great strength. His hinder thighs or gastains, should be well let down even to the middle joint, thick, brawny, full, and swelling, this being a great sign of strength and goodness; lank and slender thighs show disability and weakness. From the thigh bone to the hock it should be pretty long, but short from the hock to the pastern. Observe the middle joint behind, and if it be nothing but skin and bone, veins and sinews, rather a little bending than too straight, it is perfect as it should be; on the contrary should it have chaps or sores on the inward bought, or bending, it is a fallender.

A narrow-chested horse can never have a good body, nor breathe well, and such horses as have straight ribs, and are at the same time great feeders, will soon distend their bellies to such a degree that it will be impossible for their entrails to be contained within their ribs, but they will press down, and form what is called a cow's belly.   A man should never purchase a light-bellied and fiery horse, because he will quickly destroy himself; but in this case, care should be taken to distinguish between fierceness and vigour.   Light-bellied horses are apt to be troubled with spavins.

SPAVINS.

A permanent cure of the spavin can rarely be made, and we consider a spavined horse as a ruined one.

A spavin is a lump or swelling on the inside of the hock, that benumbs the limbs and destroys the free use of the hind legs. It makes the horse go extremely lame, and causes him much agony.

Should the joint be generally swelled all over, he must have had a blow or bruise; if in any particular part, as in the pot, or hollow part, or on the inside, the vein full and proud, and the swelling soft, it is a blood spavin; you cannot therefore take too much care in examining the hocks of delicate horses, for let the swelling appear ever so small upon the flat of the lower part of the hock, within side, though the horse may not limp, you ought to be apprehensive that in time, and with but little labour, the spavin will increase on him.

The fat spavin comes almost in the same place as the other, but is larger.

A third kind is the ox spavin, and this is thought the worst of the three.   If the swelling be hard, it is a bone spavin ; you should examine a horse thoroughly, there-fore, before you buy him, and, in particular, see if all the joints of his legs move with equal freedom. Most horses that have the bone spavin are very apt to start when you go to take up their legs, and will hardly let you touch them with your hand ; examine them well, therefore, with your eye, and see if between the fetlock and the crown, the leg descends even and smooth ; for if you see any protuberance between the flesh and the skin, that looks like a sort of knot or kernel, you have found the defect.

In purchasing a horse, much regard should be paid to his bringing up his hind parts well, for a spavined horse never makes a full step with the leg that is affected.

A CURB.

If you observe the swelling to be exactly before the knuckle, it is a curb, which is an accident that may happen in different manners ; such as a strain in work-ing, slipping his foot in a hole, or in marshy ground, &c., out of which he pulls it with pain, and by that means wrenches his hock, without dislocating any thing, and yet, without speedy care he may be lamed.

A RAT'S TAIL.

There is also a defect which is more common in the ind than the fore legs, though the latter are not quite xempt from it, and it is called the Rat's Tail, and is thus known. When you see, from the hind part of the fetlock, up along the nerves, a kind of line or channel that separates the hair to both sides, this is a rat's tail ;

and in summer there appears a kind of small dry scab along this channel; and in winter there issues out a humidity, like the water from the legs. A horse may work notwithstanding this disorder, for it seldom lames him, it sometimes occasions a stiffness in the legs, and makes them trot like foxes, without bending their joints. The hind legs should be lean, clean, flat, and sinewy; for if fat, they will not bear labour; if swelled, the grease is molten into them; if scabbed above the pasterns, it is the scratches, and if he has chaps under the pasterns he has what is generally called the Rains. If he has a good buttock, his tail cannot stand ill, but will be broad, high, flat, and couched a little inward.

A WALK AND TROT IN HAND.

Having with care examined the horse, let him be run in hand a gentle trot; by this you will soon perceive if he is lame or not. Make the man lead him by the end of the bridle, as in this case you cannot be deceived by the man's being too near him. The far fore leg, and near hind leg, or the near fore leg, and far hind leg, should move and go forward at one and the same time; and in this motion, the nearer the horse takes his limbs from the ground, the opener, the evener, and the shorter is his pace.

FORGING.

If he takes up his feet slovenly, it shows stumbling or lameness; to tread narrow, or cross, shows interfering, or failing; to step uneven, shows weariness, and if he treads long, you may be apprehensive he forges, by which I mean, that when he walks, or trots, he strikes the toes of his hind feet against the corners of his shoes before, which occasions a clattering noise as you ride; and this proceeds generally from the weakness of his fore legs, he not having strength in them to raise them up sufficiently quick to make way for the hind ones. A horse of this kind is not near so serviceable as the horse exempt from it, and the dealers, to get rid of him, will make abundance of pretences: if he has been just shoed, they will say the farrier has put him on too long shoes; if his shoes are old, they will tell you he is just come off a long journey, and is much fatigued; you must not therefore be over credulous to any thing a jockey or dealer affirms, for what they say in this manner, is too often with intent to deceive; and it is very certain that a horse who forges can never be sure-footed, any more than one who has tottering or bow-legs.

WALK AND TROT MOUNTED.

On his being mounted, see him walk. Observe his mouth, that he pulls fair, not too high, nor bearing down; then stand behind him, and see if he goes narrower before than behind, as every horse that goes well on his legs goes in that manner. Take notice that he brushes not by going too close; a certain sign of his cutting, and tiring in travelling. Have nothing to do with that horse who throws his legs confusedly about, and crosses them before: This you may observe by standing exactly before or behind him, as he is going along. In his trot he should point his fore legs well, without clambering, nor yet as if he were afraid; and that he throws well in his hind legs, which will enable him to support his trot, and shoot his fore parts forewards.

A CANTER OR GALLOP.

In his canter, observe he does not fret, but goes cool
in this pace; and in his gallop, he should take his feet
nimbly from the ground, and not raise them too high,
but that he stretches out his fore legs and follows nimbly
with his hind ones, and that he cuts not under his knee,
(which is called the swift or speedy cut) that he crosses
not, nor claps one foot on another, and ever leads with
his far fore foot, and not with the near one. If he gallops round, and raises his fore feet, he may be said to
gallop strongly, but not swiftly; and if he labour his
feet confusedly, and seems to gallop painfully, it shows
some hidden lameness; for in all his paces, you should
particularly observe that his limbs are free, without the
least stiffness.

TOTTERING LEGS.

Now that he has been well exercised in those different
paces, it is your time to examine for an infirmity, not
easily discovered, and that is what we call Tottering legs;
you cannot perceive it till after a horse has galloped for
some time, and then, by letting him rest a little you will
see his legs tremble under him, which is the disorder we
mean: however handsome soever the legs of such a
horse may be, he never can stand well on them; you
are therefore not to mind what the jockey says when he
talks of the beauty of the limbs, for if you oblige him
to gallop the horse, or fatigue him pretty much, (which
is commonly done in order to try the creature's bottom)
you will in all likelihood discover this defect, unless you
suffer the groom to gallop him to the stable door and

put him up in a moment, which he will certainly
endeavour to do, if he is conscious of it, while the
master has another horse ready to show you, in order
to take off your attention from what he is afraid you
should see.

Thus having to the best of our judgment, gone
through every requisite observation relative to the
purchase of a horse, studiously avoiding its being drawn
into an unnecessary length, yet at the same time being
as careful to avoid an affected brevity; the gentlemen
to whom many of our observations are familiar, will
please to observe, that we have endeavoured, as much
as possible, to write for the information of the person
entirely unacquainted with the qualifications which form
a complete horse; in the purchase of which, the person
should particularly consider the end for which he buys,
whether for running, hunting, travelling, draught, or
burden; and it is therefore almost unnecessary to
remind him, that the biggest and strongest are fittest for
strong occasions, burdens, draught or double carriage,
as the middle size is for hunting, pleasure, general em-
ployments, and the least for summer hackney.

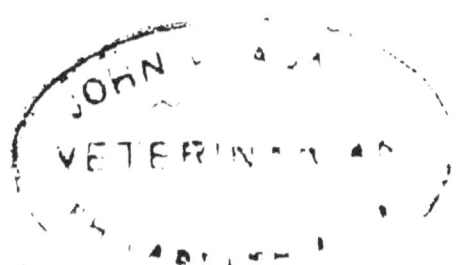

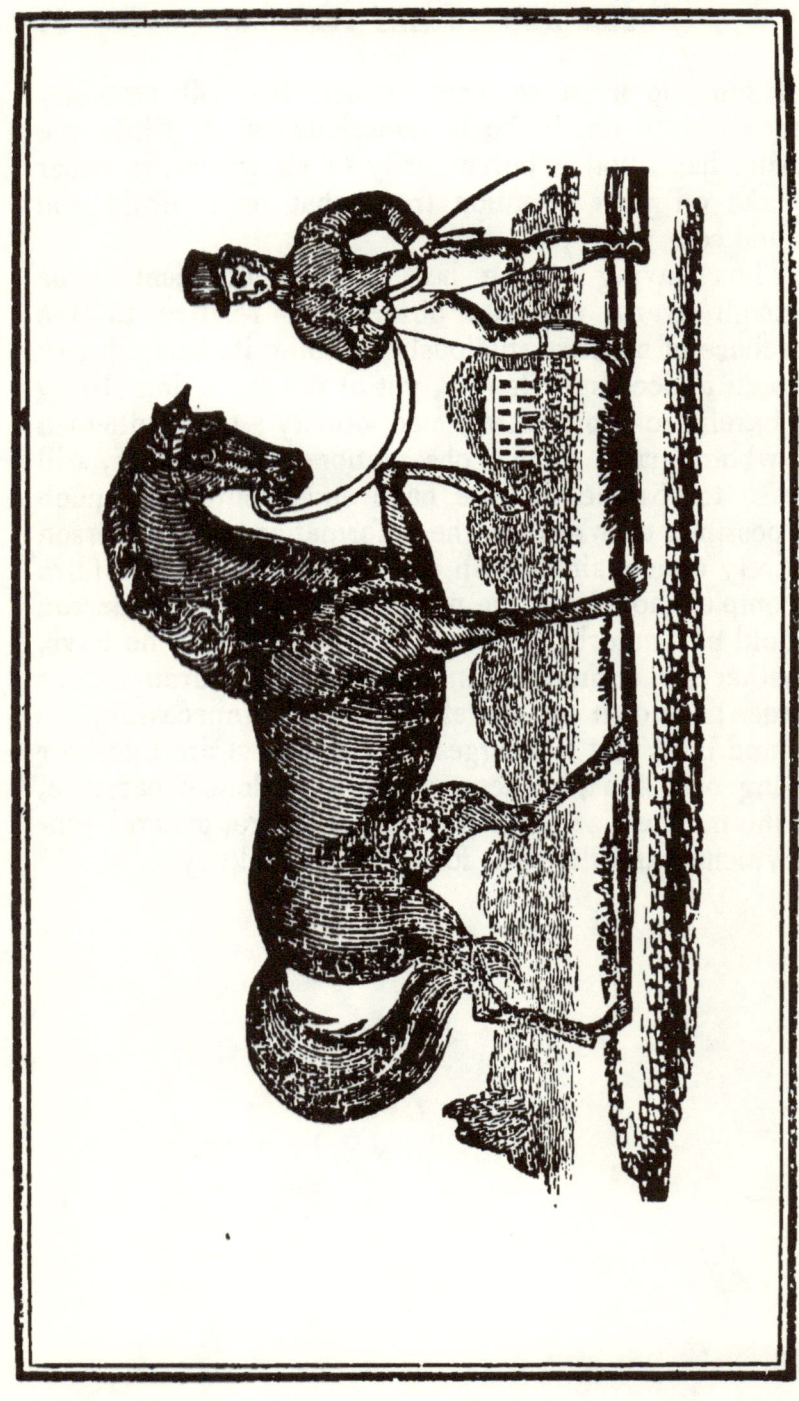

POCKET FARRIER.

TRY BEFORE YOU BUY.

If you meet with a horse you like and are desirous of buying him; do not fall in love with him before you ride him, for though he may be handsome, he may start or stumble.

TO DISCOVER A STUMBLER.

If you go to buy of one that knows you, it is not unreasonable to desire to ride him for an hour. If refused, you may expect he has some faults; if not, mount him at the door of the stable where he stands; let him neither feel your spurs, nor see your whip; mount him easily, and when seated, go gently off with a loose rein, which will make him careless; and if he is a stumbler, he will discover himself presently, especially if the road in which you ride him be any way rough.

The best horse indeed may stumble, (a young one of spirit, if not properly broken in, will frequently; and yet, if he moves nimbly upon the bit, dividing his legs true, he may become a very good saddle horse) the best horse, I say, may stumble, but if he springs out, when he stumbles, as if he feared your whip or spur, depend upon it, he is an old offender. A horse should never be struck for stumbling or starting: the provocation, I confess, is great; but the fear of corrrection makes him worse.

39

In the purchase of a horse, examine four things, his teeth, his eyes, his legs and his wind.

TO KNOW HIS AGE.

Every treatise on farriery has instructed us to know a horse's age, by the mark in his mouth; but not one in five hundred (a dealer excepted) can retain it in his mind. Let this then be sufficient: with your finger and thumb, raise his upper lip, and if his teeth shut close, you may suppose him young; but if they point forward, and the upper and under edges do not meet even, you may suspect he is old. And the longer his teeth are, (the gums being dry and shrunk from them, looking yellow and rusty) the older he is.

There are some exceptions to the above rule, but by a due attention you will seldom be deceived.

You may indeed examine his tush, and if it be pointed and grooved, that is, hollowish on the inside, he cannot be judged to be above seven years old. Crafty jockeys will sometimes burn holes in the teeth, to make them appear young, which they call bishoping, but a discerning eye will soon discover the cheat. Mares have no tushes, so that it is more difficult to know their age, but if the roof of the mouth be fleshy, and almost as proud as the teeth, she is young.

EYES.

If a horse's eyes are lively and clear, and you can see to the bottom, and the image of your face be reflected from thence, and not from the surface of the eye, they are good; but if muddy, cloudy or coal black, they are bad.

LEGS.

If, his knees are not broken, nor stand bending and trembling forward, (which is called knuckling) his legs may be good ; but if he steps short and digs his toes in the ground, it is a sign he will knuckle. In short, if the hoof be pretty flat and not curled, you need not fear a founder.

WIND.

If his flanks beat even and slow, his wind may be good ; but if they heave double and irregular, or if (while he stands in the stable) he blows at the nostrils, as if he had just been galloping, they are signs of a broken wind. Deceitful dealers have a draught which they sometimes give, to make a horse breathe regularly in the stable : the surest way to judge of his wind, is to give him a good brushing gallop, and it is ten to one, if his wind be broken or even touched, that he will cough and wheeze very much, and no medicine can prevent his doing so.

REGIMEN FOR A BROKEN WIND.

This is a disease in every respect similar to the asthma in the human species. The symptoms are a hollow cough, which is increased by exercise, and attended with a wheezing, or difficulty of breathing, and a working of the flanks. This disorder is commonly brought on by voracious feeding, which distends the stomach inordinately ; by violent exercise when the belly is full ; by being driven into water when he is sweated and hot ; or from a cold, not well cured. Horses that eat their litter, and what other hard substances they come near, are predisposed to broken-wind, by the great distension of the stomach and inability of inspiring a sufficiency of air to fill the lungs.

Cure there is none for broken-wind, but a horse that has it may be rendered very useful by proper attention to regimen. Of course, particular care should be taken to avoid exposing him to *fresh cold*, and not push him too hard on a full stomach. The horse should have good nourishment, but condensed in bulk—not quantity enough to distend his bowels, but rich and nutritious, what there is of it. Water should be given him sparingly. Give him rather plentifully of corn, but little hay, and that little wet with water. Some advise that water given him should every day be impregnated with half an ounce of salt-petre and two drachms of sal-ammoniac.

When the cough is particularly troublesome, or the animal seems to labour much in respiration, give the following. Dried squills, powdered, 1 drachm; gum ammoniacum, 3 drachms; opium, 10 drachms; with mucilage sufficient to form the ball.

Broken-winded horses have been greatly relieved by drinking daily a bucket of water poured off from quick-lime. A horse supplied with water thus prepared, and kept in the stable five or six weeks, will recover his wind in a great degree and his cough will be much abated.

A DRAUGHT HORSE.

A horse with thick shoulders and a broad chest, laden with flesh, hanging too forward, and heavily projecting over his knees and feet, is fitter for a collar than a saddle.

A SADDLE HORSE.

A horse with thin shoulders, and a flat chest, whose fore-feet stand boldly forward and even, his neck rising semicircular from the points of those thin shoulders to his head, may justly be said to have a light forehand and be fitter for a saddle than a collar. As most horses in the hands of farmers are drawn while they are young, which, notwithstanding their make, occasions them to move heavily, if you desire a nimble-footed horse, choose one that has never drawn.

In buying a horse enquire into four other things, viz. biting, kicking, stopping, and starting.

STARTING AND SHYING.

Starting is when a horse grows wanton or skittish, and takes every object he sees to be different from what it is. It is one of the worst habits a horse can have, and tends to reduce his value much, for as good a rider as a person may be, he cannot be on his guard against a starting horse.

If you would ascertain that a horse starts, mount him yourself, ride first slowly and then fast towards and along by objects that you discover are offensive to his eye, and you will soon assure yourself whether or not he has this bad habit.

Horses that have been kept pampered in the stable for some time, without regular airings or exercise, are liable to start when first ridden out, but are in general easily cured.

Some horses will observe particularly all objects they meet, and sidle a little, or shy from it, but a starting horse that all at once leaps from one side to the other, is neither safe nor agreeable, and we would advise the owner of such an animal, if he has any consideration for his own neck, to get rid of him as soon as possible, for whoever undertakes to break a horse of this trick endangers his life to an imminent degree.

When riding a horse of this kind, however, in all cases treat him with the utmost gentleness ; neither beat him nor speak harshly to him during his fright, but make him advance gently to the object—this treatment will in time (with some horses) give them confidence and free them from their foolish fears.

TO CURE THE SPLINTS.

The splint is a fixed hard excrescence or knob, grow-ing upon the flat of the in or outside (and sometimes both) of the shank bone ; a little under, and not far from the knee, and may be seen and felt.

Splints when buried within the tendons are apt to lame a horse seriously ; but, if situated on the plain bone, unless very large, they seldom do injury ; and if a splint be early attended to it is not very difficult to remove.

Some practitioners rub the splint with a round stick till the part is almost raw, and then touch it with oil of origanum.   Others lay on a pitch plaster, with a small quantity of sublimate or arsenic, to corrode and eat the substance away.   Others again use butter of antimony, or oil of vitriol, and some tincture of cantharides.   All of which methods have at times succeeded ; but they are most, if not all, apt to leave an ugly scar behind, with the loss of all the hair on the part.   Blaine recom-mends the swelling to be rubbed night and morning for five or six days, with a drachm of mercurial ointment, rubbing it well in; after which apply a blister, and at the end of a fortnight or three weeks another.

THE SPAVIN.

The Spavin is of the same nature, and appears, in like manner, on the instep bone behind, not far below the hock.

The destruction of the horse has often occurred by letting out the contents of these tumours. This must not be, but the sides of the tumours must be strengthened by pressure or by stimulants. The best stimulant is the strong liquid blister of the Veterinary Pharmacy, as— Spanish flies, in gross powder, 1 oz; oil of origanum, 2 drachms; oil of turpentine, 4 oz; olive oil, 2 oz; steep the flies in the turpentine three weeks, strain off and add the oil. Bandages assist greatly, when well applied.

WINDGALLS.

Windgalls are several little swellings just above the fetlock-joints of all the four legs; they seem, when felt, to be full of wind or jelly, but they never lame a horse; the splint and spavin always do. They all three proceed from one and the same cause, which is hard riding, travelling too far in one day, or carrying too great a weight when young.

Blistering is the general remedy applied to these. In most cases, where there is no greater inconvenience arising from them than what is visible to the eye, it will be better to let them alone, as there have been many instances of horses being totally lamed and rendered unfit for service by wounding the tendons in an operation.

SETTING OUT ON A JOURNEY.

Having premised thus much of the qualities necessary to a good horse, we now proceed to give such directions in regard to a journey on horseback as will be found to be of the utmost importance to the traveller.

Whenever you intend to travel, hunt, or only ride out for the air, let your horse's feet be examined some time before, to see that his shoes are all fast and sit easy on his feet, for on that depends the pleasure and safety of your journey.

DIRECTIONS FOR MOUNTING.

Before you mount, look round your horse, to see if his bridle, curb, saddle, and girths are all fitted in their proper places. Always accustom your horse to stand firm and without a motion, till you are fixed in your seat and your clothes be adjusted.

DIRECTIONS FOR GOING.

When you would have him go, teach him to move, by pressing close your knees, or speaking to him, without using whip or spur; for a horse will learn any thing, and a good quality may as easily be taught him as a bad one.

CORRECTION ILL-TIMED.—CORRECTION
WELL-TIMED.—AN EASY REIN.

Most men whip and spur a horse, to make him go faster, before they bid him; but it is cruel treatment, to beat a generous creature, before you have signified your mind to him, (by some token which he may be taught to understand) who would obey you if he knew your pleasure; it is time enough to correct him when he re- fuses, or resists you. Do not haul his head about with too tight a rein, it deadens his mouth; besides, he will carry you safer, and take better care of his steps with an easy hand, than a heavy one; much depends on the quietness of the bridle hand. Keep in your elbows steady, and you cannot hurt his mouth. Again, nothing discovers a bad horseman (even at a distance) so much as throwing his legs and arms about; for it is easier to the horse and rider, and he can carry you further by ten miles a day, when you sit as steady upon him as if you were a part of himself.

CUTTING.

 If he cuts either before or behind, look that his shoes stand not with an edge beyond the hoof, and feel that the clinches of the nails lie close; but if cutting proceeds from interfering, that is, crossing his legs in his trot, it is a natural infirmity and can only be a little helped by care. Horses will sometimes cut, when leg-weary, which they will recover of by rest. If you would not have a horse that cuts, buy not one who stands with his toes turned outwards, nor one who, in trotting, carries his legs too near each other.

LAMENESS.—A POULTICE.

If (as he stands in the stable) you observe him to point one foot forwarder than the other, either before or behind, seeming to bear no weight on it, you may rea- sonably conclude he is not easy: if the shoes is the cause, the farrier can remove it presently, but if the foot is not hurt by some unknown accident, make *a poultice of any sort of greens, such as lettuce, cabbage, marsh-mallow leaves, turnip tops, or turnips themselves, the best of all; boil them tender, squeeze the water out, chop them in a wooden bowl, with two or three ounces of hog's lard or butter;* put this poultice into a cloth, and tie his foot in it all night, as hot as you can.

In the morning, when the farrier comes to take off his shoe, he will find his hoof cut soft and easy, so that he will soon discover (in paring with his buttrice) whether he is pricked or bruised.

GRAVELLED.

A misfortune that sometimes happens to a horse on a journey : it consists in little pebbles getting between the shoe and the hoof and settling there, so as to get to the quick and fester. The only way to cure it is to take off the shoe, and then draw the place with a drawing-iron till you come to the quick; this done, pick out the gravel and squeeze out the matter and blood that is found collected there. Then wash the parts well with simple tincture of myrrh, and stop up the hole with hurds wet in the same. After which let the shoe be carefully put on again, and in two or three times thus dressing, he will get well. But do not travel, or work him, before he is so, nor let his foot go into the wet, which would greatly retard his cure.

PRICKED.

A horse's foot is pricked by having a nail driven too far into it at the time of shoeing, so as to reach the quick, or press the vein, and cause lameness. When a

horse is pricked in the foot, whether it be by the negligence of the farrier in driving the nails, or from any
other accident, they should be drawn out immediately
on the discovery thereof; otherwise the wound will fester
and break out into an open sore.   It is easily discerned
that a horse is pricked by his going lame, but with more
certainty by trying round the hoof with a pair of pincers, for when you come to the aggrieved place he will
cringe and draw away his foot.   The shoe should at
once be taken off, and the horse turned out to grass, if
possible, without applying anything external to it.   But
if turning him out cannot be complied with, rub frequently on his foot a little ointment of elder.

LAME IN THE HEEL OR HOOF.—THE CURE.

If your horse is lame with a hole in his heel, or any
part of his hoof, be it ever so deep, occasioned by an
over-reach of his hind-foot, or a tread of another horse,
though gravel be in it, put his foot into the aforesaid
poultice, [*See page* 53.] and repeat it mornings and evenings, till it is well; for it will suck it out, fill it again with
sound flesh, and make the hoof grow over it, much
sooner than any other method or medicine whatsoever.

CUTS, TREADS, AND BRUISES CURED.

All cuts, treads and bruises are cured by this poultice;
not only quick and sure, but without leaving any mark.

THE HORSE-OINTMENT.

Into a clean pipkin, that holds about a quart, put the
bigness of a pullet's egg of yellow rosin; when it is
melted over a middling fire, add the same quantity of

*bees' wax ; when that is melted, put in half a pound
of hog's lard ; when it is dissolved, put in two ounces
of honey; when that is dissolved, put in half a pound
of common turpentine ; keep it gently boiling, stirring
it with a stick all the time ; when the turpentine is dissolved, put in two ounces of verdigris ; you must take
off the pipkin, (else it will rise into the fire in a moment) set it on again, and give it two or three wambles
and strain it through a coarse sieve, into a clean vessel
for use, and throw the dregs away.*

This is an extraordinary ointment for a wound or
bruise in flesh or hoof, broken knees, galled backs,
bites, cracked heels, mallanders, or when you geld a
horse, to heal and keep the flies away ; nothing takes
fire out of a burn or scald in human flesh so soon ; I
have had personal experience of it. I had it out of
Degrey, but finding it apt to heal a wound at the top,
before the bottom was found, I improved it, by adding an
ounce of verdigris.

HEAT-BALLS.

If, upon a journey, any little bumps called heat-balls
should rise on your horse's shoulders or any part of
him ; upon coming to your inn, order the hostler to rub
them often with hot vinegar, which will disperse them.
They are owing to the heat of the body in hard riding.
If they are not dispersed, they will burst and look ugly,
and it will be some time before the hair comes on upon
the part again.

SWELLED AND CRACKED HEELS.—CURE.

If his legs and heels should swell and crack and become stiff and sore, so that he can hardly be got out of

the stable in the morning, and perhaps did not lie down all night ; you may travel on, but walk him for the first mile or two, very gently, till the swelling falls, and he begins to feel his legs.

When you end the day's journey, wash his sore legs with warm water, and a great deal of soap ; or foment his heels, (first cutting away the hair very close) with old urine, pretty warm, for a quarter of an hour, by dipping a woolen cloth, or an old stocking, into the urine, squeezing it, and then applying it to the part affected, having first well washed it with the urine. You may then prepare the poultice, as in page 53, and tie it on hot, as soon as it can be got ready, letting it stay on all night. Feed him as usual, and offer him warm water in the house. About nine or ten o'clock (that is, an hour or two after he is put up for all night, and fed) give him a ball composed of *half an ounce of ethiops mineral. Ditto of balsam of sulphur terib. Ditto of diopente or powdered aniseeds mixed and made into a ball with honey or treacle.* You may give him a pint of warm ale after it.

Do not stir him out of the stable on any account whatever, till you mount him the next morning for your journey, and give him a draught of warm water in the stable before you set out (that being proper on account of the ball.) When you are on the road, he may drink water as usual.

The next night omit the ball, but continue the poultice.

The third night give the second ball.

GREASING HEELS.

The fifth night give the third ball, and still continue the poultice till his heels are well: but if you can get no sort of poulticing, then, melt hog's lard, or butter, and with a rabbit's foot or a rag, grease his heels with it very hot.

If he is a young horse, and the distemper new, you will hear no more of it; but if he is old, and hath had it a long time on him, it will require further repetition.

N. B.   During this operation, you must not gallop on the road, but ride moderately, for sweating will retard the cure.   You must consider, that wet weather, and wet roads are by no means proper for this regimen.

Travelling indeed is an improper time for this cure, except in cases of necessity; if you can give your horse rest, his heels will get well sooner by turning him out to grass, and renewing the poultices; but he should be kept in the stable while he takes the medicine.

If the greasy poultice does not effect a cure, which may sometimes be the case; after fomenting the legs with urine, anoint his heels well with the following ointment warm every night. *Take ten eggs, boil them very hard, put them in cold water; when cold, separate the yolks from the whites, put all the yolks into a frying pan, bruise them with a spoon over the fire, till they turn black and yield a fetid oil, which decant off, and mix it, while warm, with two ounces of honey, and two ounces of white lead in powder, and then keep it for use.   It should be beaten into a horse's hoof, with a fire shovel.* The heels in the day time should be constantly well rubbed.—This ointment exceeds any thing that can be applied for a burn or scald in the human body, if applied soon after the accident, and the part affected be anointed for an hour after, by times, with a feather.

I have often cured a horse of greasy heels by giving him only an ounce and a half of saltpetre pounded fine, or dissolved and mixed with his corn, morning and evening. But this must be continued for a month or more, till his legs are well; but they should be kept washed as above. If you give a horse five or six pounds of saltpetre, in this manner, it will not hurt him, it will free him from all sorts of humours, and put him into excellent spirits.

MALLENDER, AND CURE.

The mallender is a crack in the bend of the knee, it oozes a sharp humour like that at the heels or frush; a horse dare not step out for fear of tearing it wider; it is so painful it takes away his belly; it makes him step short, and stumble much.

The same method, medicine, greasing and poulticing, which you used for swelled or cracked heels, will cure it.

SELLENDER, AND CURE.

The sellender is a crack in the bend of the hock; and must be cured with the same things, and after the same manner.

SORE BACK, AND CURE.

If the saddle bruises his back, and makes it swell, a greasy dish-clout laid on hot, and a cloth or rag over it, bound on, a quarter of an hour (with a surcingle) and repeated once or twice, will sink it flat. If it is slight, wash it with a little water and salt only :~but you must have the saddle altered, that it press not upon the tender part, for a second bruise will be worse than the first. If his furniture does not fit and sit easy, it will damp him; but if nothing wound or hurt him, he will travel with courage.

5 *

ADVICE FOR WATERING.

Make it a standing rule to water on the way before you arrive at the baiting place, be it noon or night; if there is no water by the way, do not (when once you have entered the stable) suffer any man to lead him out to a river or horse-pond, to wash his legs or drink, but give him warm water in the house.

If you ride moderately, you ought to let your horse drink at any time on the way; you may trust him, he will not take harm, but always refresh himself; but if he has been long without water, and is hot, he will then overdrink himself, and it may spoil him, because a load of cold water greedily swallowed while he is hot, will certainly chill and deaden the tone of the stomach; but two or three go-downs are really necessary to cool his mouth, and may be allowed him at any time on the road.

DIFFICULTY OF STALING.

Sometimes a horse cannot stale, and will be in great pain; to ease him, *take half an ounce of aniseeds beaten fine in a mortar, one handful of parsley roots, boil these in a quart of old strong beer, and strain it off, and give it him warm.*

Staling (a suppression thereof) may be brought on a horse by being kept high and having too little exercise, as well as by hard travelling. The signs of this complaint are as follows,—the creature will roll and tumble about with the violence of the pain under which he labours, and while on his legs will continually be straining and putting himself in a position to stale, but without being able to do anything more than void a few drops, or perhaps none at all.

DIABETES.

A morbid copiousness of urine, or making water in too great quantities, which disorder is very common in horses, and frequently terminates in their death.   It is generally the result of old disorders, such as surfeits and excessive hard driving.   The horse soon loses flesh and appetite, his hair grows rough and staring.   A horse thus affected should not be allowed too much water.   If the following remedy is applied when the disease first makes its appearance, by proper attention the cure will be almost certain.   One drachm of opium, two drachms of asafœtida, two drachms powdered ginger, one ounce powdered red oak bark, with enough of any kind of syrup to make two balls for one dose, which must be given to him three times a week, and especial care taken not to let him drink much water.

Some persons use the following receipt: one ounce gum arabic, one pint of red wine, and a pint of water, mixed and given as a drench three times a week.

Moderate exercise and nourishing food will assist much in effecting the cure.

SURFEIT AND MANGE.

The surfeit is common among horses that have not been judiciously treated.   Sudden changes from warmth to cold frequently cause it.   Over-feeding also produces it.   When a horse is surfeited, his coat will stare and look rueful, notwithstanding all proper care has been taken to keep him clean, and the skin will be found full of scales and scurf, lying thick like meal among the hair, and constantly supplied with a fresh succession on that being cleared away; the horse is disturbed by a constant itching; the hair of both the mane and tail rubs off, and the little that remains stands erect.

Surfeit, when it first appears is easily removed by a cooling purgative; but if the pulse be high he should be bled also. Promote perspiration by means of a diaphoretic. If the animal be fat he must be reduced. Give a mash of one gallon of bran, a table spoonful of saltpetre, a table spoonful of sulphur, and a quart of hot sassafras tea, well mixed together, three times within a week. When the mash is taken, be careful not to let him drink for six hours. Change his litter frequently, keep his stable clean, and do not permit him to get wet. An ointment of hog's lard and sulphur applied once a day on the places where the surfeit appears worst, will be found to be of great benefit. Remember that his food during this treatment must be light and easily digested, and fail not to observe towards him the kindest treatment.

The *Mange* sometimes succeeds an ill-cured surfeit; and is moreover an original disease, arising from beastliness, hard living, ill-usage, and the consequent depravation of the humours. It partakes of the nature of itch in man, is communicable by means of the touch, by using the same harness, clothing, &c., and probably by standing in the same stall that a diseased horse may have left. The horse, as he is with the surfeit, is constantly rubbing and biting himself.

There are at present a variety of prescriptions in use. The following is effectual. Bleed copiously, and during a week give him three mashes like that for the surfeit; and rub the part affected twice a day with an ointment of hog's lard and brimstone in equal parts. Keep his stable scrupulously clean and furnished with a nice bed of straw.

HARD RIDING.

If you ride hard, and go in hot, your horse will be off his stomach; then is your time to guard against a surfeit, which is always attended with the grease, the farcy, or both; the symptons are *staring of the coat,* and *hide-bound.*

Staring of the coat will appear the very next morning. To prevent which, as soon as you dismount rub him well, cover him, pick his feet, throw a handful or two of beans before him, and litter him deep. Go immediately and boil, for a cordial, *half a pound of aniseeds in a quart of ale, pour it upon half a pound of honey, into a bowl or bason; brew it about, till it is almost as cold as blood, then give it* (with a horn) *seeds and all.*

To cure him, feed as usual, but keep him warmly clothed; give him warm water that night, and next morning. A mash will do well that night, and lest the cordial should not have force enough to carry off the surfeit, you must give him (after all, and just before bed time) one of those balls directed in page 51.

To prevent stiffness: supple and wash his legs with greasy dish-wash, or water and soap, as hot as a man can bear his hand in it, with a dish-clout, and by no means take him out of the stable that night. Grease his hoofs, and stop his feet with the following ball; it is safe and innocent: *two or three handfuls of bran put into a little saucepan with as much grease of any kind as will moisten it. Let it cool, and put a ball of it into each fore foot.*

Cover each ball with a little tow or straw, and put a couple of splints over that, to keep it in all night. This do every night if you please throughout your journey, it is good at any time if he lie still; but these balls are

not necessary in the winter, or when the roads are full
of water.

Ever avoid all stuffings made of cow-dung, clay and
urine, which you will find ready mixed in a tub, in the
custody of almost every hostler; such cold stuffings
benumb the feet to that degree, that the horse fumbles
and steps short for two or three miles, till he gets a little
warmth and feels his feet again.

HIDE-BOUND.

A horse is said to be hide-bound when the skin sticks
so closely to the back and ribs that it cannot be laid hold
of, or raised by the hand without great difficulty.

The treatment in this case should be plenty of light
food and a stable kept perfectly clean, with strict attention to keeping him supplied with a fresh litter. Bleed
him, take from his neck half a gallon; and at night
give him a mash made the same as that given for the
surfeit and mange.   .

On the second day, take two spoonfuls of copperas;
one quart of warm sassafras tea; and one tea spoonful of saltpetre; mix and give them as a drench. Have
the horse rubbed well, and he will be entirely relieved in
a few days.

THE SHOULDER-SLIP.

The shoulder wrench or slip may happen to a horse
in various ways, as by stopping and turning too suddenly
upon unlevel ground, or by sliding or slipping down,
either in the stable or the field, or by running suddenly
through a door or gate, &c. If, while on the road, you
wrench his shoulder, mix *two ounces of the oil of spike*

with one ounce of the oil of swallows, and half an ounce of turpentine, and, with your hands, rub a little of it all over the shoulder. It will be best to warm the oils well with a broad-mouthed fire shovel, or plate of iron, hot. Then bleed him, and let him rest two days. This will cure a slight strain. Should he continue lame, you may travel on, but slowly, and he will grow well upon the road; but repeat the oils.

STIFLE.—THE CURE.

If you strain your horse in the stifle, a little bone upon the thigh bone, above the inside bend of the hock; (you find such another in a leg of mutton) the turnip poultice will infallibly cure it, but you may rub in the oils first, as ordered for the shoulder-slip. By its situation, you will find a difficulty to keep the poultice on, yet it may be done with a few yards of list.

If it is not well, or very much mended, in two or three days, examine the hip, perhaps you may find it there; but this may be cured by oiling, as in a shoulder-slip, for the poultice cannot be fastened on there.

A CLAP IN THE BACK SINEWS.

When lameness arises from a clap in the back sinews, which is a relaxation of the sinews from a strain, take a spoonful or two of hog's lard, or rather goose-grease, melt it in a saucepan, and rub it into the back sinew very hot, from the bend of the knee to the fetlock; make (as you are directed in page 53) a turnip poultice and tie it on hot, from the fetlock to above the knee, and let it stay on all night; thus, first tie the cloth about the fetlock, then put in the poultice, and raise the cloth and the poultice together, till you get it above the bend of the knee; twisting the list or string round his leg as you rise, and fasten it above the knee; take it off in the morning, and put on a fresh one; at night do the same. Two or three of these poultices will cure a new strain; five or six, an old one.

HOW TO KNOW A SHOULDER-SLIP, FROM A STRAIN IN THE BACK SINEWS.

This lameness, by ignorant farriers, is frequently taken for a shoulder-slip; and in consequence of this, they proceed to blowing, boring, and rowelling, and thus make your horse useless for a long time. Be not imposed on; be sure it is in his shoulder, before you admit the operation.

If it is in his shoulder, he will drag his toe on the ground, as he walks.

If in the back sinew, he will lift it off and step short, though downright lame.

There does not happer above one shoulder-slip, to fifty back-sinew strains.

A COLD—A RUNNING OF THE EYES AND NOSTRILS.

You may know if your horse has caught cold by a running at his eyes, and a little gleeting at his nostrils; though it is impossible to know exactly how he came by it; (for standing near a hole, a window or door, a damp new-built stable, and many other ways may do it) yet I would warn you against one practice in particular, too much in use, which seldom fails to give a horse cold.

That is, taking him out of a warm stable, and riding him into a river or horse-pond, at an unseasonable hour, either too late or too early. A horse should never be taken out of a warm stable on a journey, till you mount him for travel.

A CAUTION TO PREVENT FOUNDERING ON THE ROAD.

It is the opinion of most grooms, that a horse heats his legs and feet upon a hard road, especially if he is a heavy horse, or carries a great weight, and that he should be refreshed and cooled by washing. To which I agree; but then it must be with warm water, for that cools best. This will not only open the pores, and make his legs perspire, but it will clear his fetlock joints best of any gravel that may get in within the wrinkles, and thus fret and inflame his legs; cold water naturally contracts the skin, and binds any gravel, there may chance to be, the firmer. Stop his feet also with the ball directed in page 57, but make it pretty warm.

Note.—A horse in this case ought to have a large stall, that he may stretch his legs. Young horses require larger stalls than old ones; for an accustomed old horse will ease himself in a stall of five feet wide, as well as in one of two yards.

A COUGH.—THE CURE.

If (after a day or two) you perceive a running at his eyes, and a little gleeting at his nostrils, you may expect to hear him cough. In that case, take a pint of blood from his neck, in a morning, (a horse will travel notwithstanding, if you do not exceed it) and at noon give an additional feed, to make amends for the loss of blood.

At night give him a mash, over and above his usual allowance. The next night give him the aniseed cordial as before.

If his cough continues three days, you must take another pint of blood from his neck, and try to remove it with abler medicines. Therefore, to keep it off his lungs, give him, just before you go to bed,—*Liquorice powder, an ounce. Sweet oil, a spoonful. Æthiops mineral, an ounce. Balsam of sulphur, half an ounce.* Made into a ball with a little honey.

Clothe and keep him warm. Repeat the ball next night, which will be sufficient to cure any new-gotten cold or surfeit.

KNOTTED BETWEEN THE JAWS.—CURE.

Feel between his jaws, and if his kernels are swelled, do not let the farrier cut them out with a pair of red-hot scissors (as some of them do) but dissolve them with two or three or more turnip poultices, and continue the aniseed cordial till he is well.

If the almonds of a man's ears were down ; that is, if the glands were swelled, and a surgeon proposed to cut them out for a cure, you would treat him with great contempt for his ignorance. It is the same with respect to a horse.

Note.—The horse's throat ought to be kept warm with cloths, till the swelling is either dissolved or come to a head ; if the latter, any common farrier may open the tumour with a sharp pen-knife, and when the matter has free discharge, the wound will easily heal, by the use of *the horse ointment* applied warm.

I will next mention the eyes, for it is as bad for a horse to be blind as to be lame.

A COLD IN THE EYES.—ITS TREATMENT.— A CAUTION IN BLEEDING.

When a horse has got cold, it sometimes falls into his eyes, which you may know by the symptoms before-mentioned in page 60 ; (a running or a thick glare upon them) put your hand to his nostrils, and if you find his breath hotter than usual, it will then be necessary to take a little blood from his neck.

It is a common thing with some farriers to take two, three, and sometimes four quarts of blood away at one time. I am very much against that practice ; because you rob a horse of more animal spirits than you can restore in a long time, without much rest and high-feeding; the latter of which is diametrically opposite to the cure.

Therefore, a pint or quart at most (unless it is very thick and very hot) will be sufficient ; it is safer to take a gallon at five or six bleedings, than two quarts at once, for the reason above. Let me advise you also to take it by measure, I mean in a pint or quart pot ; for when you bleed at random upon the ground, you never can know what quantity you take, nor what quality his blood is of. From such violent methods used with igno-rance, proceed the death of half the horses in the nation.

What proof must a farrier, a groom or a coachman give of his skill, to administer to a horse a comfortable drink (as they call it) composed of diapente, long pep-per, grains of paradise, and the rest of the hot ingre-dients, at a time when his blood is boiling in his veins? It is like giving a man burnt brandy in a fever. I say, by knowing the true state of your horse's blood, you can better judge what medicines are most proper to give him.

Therefore, a pint of blood, for the first time, is enough, and you may repeat that, as you see occasion ; but you cannot easily restore (as I said) the blood and spirits you have been too lavish of.

A POULTICE FOR THE EYES.

After you have taken a pint of blood, *get a quartern loaf, hot out of the oven, cut away the crust, and put the soft inside into a linen bag large enough to cover his forehead and temples ; press it flat, and bind it on by way of poultice, as hot as may be, without scalding ; at the same time, fasten something of a cloth about his neck to keep his throat warm.* Let the poultice stay on till it is almost cold, and repeat it once or twice; then prepare the following eye-water.

EYE-WATER.

Into half a pint of rose or spring water, put one drachm of tutty, finely prepared, one drachm of white sugar-candy powdered, and half a drachm of sugar of lead. With a feather put a drop into each eye, mornings and evenings.

The next day (if needful) repeat the poultice ; and for want of a hot loaf at any time, make a poultice of bread boiled in milk, continuing the eye-water every day. You may use the turnip poultice, but you must not put grease into it.

Never let grease or oil come near the eyes.

A FILM.—THE CURE.

If a film grows over the eye, put a scruple of white vitriol and a scruple of roche-alum, both finely powdered, into half a quartern of spring-water ; and with a feather put a drop into each eye mornings and evenings, and it will eat it clean off in three days or thereabouts ; but be not prevailed on to blow flint and glass (pounded together) into the eyes ; because the sharp points of the glass wound all the tender blood-vessels, and cause an inexpressible painful inflammation, not much inferior and full as insignificant as the farriers' way of burning a thousand holes in his skin with a red-hot poker, to cure the farcy.

Gelding and docking are but little helps to bad eyes.

Blistering the temples, cutting out the haws, and taking up the veins, weaken the optics and hasten blindness.

OBSERVATIONS ON WASHY HORSES.

It is observed, some horses carry a good belly all the journey, others part with their food before it is well digested, and scour all the way ; which makes them so thin and lank, that they are ready to slip through their girts ; they are called washy. Such horses must be chiefly fed with dry meat, that is, oats and beans, and but seldom with bran. They also will eat as much or rather more than other horses, and you should feed them oftener, for being too soon empty they require it ; and if you will allow them enough, they will perform a tolerable good journey ; but I do not recommend such a one.

REMEMBER TO FEED.

If you do not gallop your horse off his wind, I will venture to say, it is not the journey that hurts him, but your neglect of him when you dismount. Consider he is tied up, and can have nothing but what is brought to

6 *

him, for he cannot help himself; and if you do not cause
him to be properly attended, a dog that wanders about
fares better than the horse that carried you so well; and
since he cannot ask for what he wants, you must supply
every thing.

DIRECTIONS FOR FEEDING.

When you end the day's journey, fill your horse's
belly as soon as you can, that he may go to rest, and
he will be the fresher for it in the morning. It is an
old observation, that young men eat and sleep better
than old; but old horses eat and sleep better than young.

Give two or three little feeds instead of a large one;
too much at once may cloy him.

A CORDIAL FOR FAINTING ON THE ROAD.

If you perceive your horse travel faintly, you may
give him at any time a pint of warm ale with a quartern
of brandy, rum or gin in it, or an ounce of diapente in
it. Diapente will comfort his bowels, drive out cold and
wind, and may cause him to carry his food the longer.

THE GRIPES.

This is a disorder to which horses are very subject,
and if improperly treated is not unlikely to prove fatal.

The attack is sudden, and is never preceded, and
seldom accompanied, by any symptoms of fever. The
horse lies down and rolls upon his back.

Some horses are naturally disposed to colic, whilst
others, with even improper treatment, are never attacked
with it. If your horse becomes restless, frequently
pawing, making many fruitless attempts to stale, and

voiding his excrement in small quantities, and looking round towards his flanks, groaning, kicking at his belly, and other marks of great agitation, you may be sure he has an attack of the gripes.

Do not bleed him (unless his breath is very hot) but clothe him warm immediately, and (with a horn) give him *half a pint of brandy, and as much sweet oil mixed;* then trot him about until he is a little warm, which will certainly cure some horses. If it does not yours, *boil one ounce of beaten pepper in a quart of milk, put half a pound of butter, and two or three ounces of salt, into a bowl or basin, and brew them together, give it rather warmer than usual;* it will purge him in half an hour or thereabouts, and perhaps remove the fit. If it does not, omit half the pepper, and give the same in quantity and quality by way of clyster, adding (as it cools) *the yolks of four eggs.*

If this has the good effect that is wished for, you must nurse him up till he gets his strength again; but if neither will do, *boil a pound of aniseeds in two quarts of ale, brew it upon a pound of honey; when it is almost cool enough, put in two ounces of diascordium,* and give it (with a horn) at three doses, allowing about half an hour between each dose.

If his fit abates, give him time to recover himself.

WORMS OR BOTTS.

If all this does not give him ease, and if you have a suspicion of worms or botts breeding in his guts, (which indeed may be the cause) for they sometimes fasten in the passage from the stomach into the great gut, and stop it; and so torment him till he dies; (I have seen it in dissections,) then give him *two ounces of Æthiops mineral made into a ball, with an ounce of the powder of aniseeds, and a spoonful of honey.*

N. B.   But you must not give this to a mare with foal.   You may bleed her in the roof of the mouth.

Dr. Morgan, of New Jersey, has the following remedy for botts.   Take a table spoonful of unslaked lime, and let it be given with the feed of the horse, at night and morning, regularly, for three, four, or five days, and it will completely expel them.

Dr. Loomis, of North Carolina, has a drench, composed of half a pint of new milk, a gill of molasses, an ounce of copperas, two spoonfuls of common salt, and half a pint of warm water.   Give this to the horse once or twice a day for a few days, and it will cure him.

THE STAGGERS, OR APOPLEXY.

Do not let your horse stand too long without exercise, it fills his belly too full of meat, and his veins too full of blood.   From hence the staggers, and many other distempers.

Upon an attack of this, the horse drops down suddenly, and lies without sense or motion, except a working of his flanks, which is occasioned by a motion of the heart and lungs, and which never ceases entirely while any spark of life remains.   The previous symptoms are, drowsiness, moist watery eyes, which sometimes appear full and inflamed, a disposition to reel, feebleness, want of appetite, an almost continual hanging down of the head ; when the horse thus falls down, the case is desperate indeed ; few, if any, recover.

There are many distinctions of this disease, as, the *sleepy* staggers, *mad* staggers.   The mad staggers is that affection of the brain, which causes the animal to kick, to tumble, and plunge about.   This and the sleepy staggers are both occasioned by a diseased stomach, brought on by inflammation of that organ, or simply by the retention of a great mass of indigestible food there and in the intestines.   Constipation attends every species of staggers, and in some cases the hardened dung may be felt by feeling at the proper part.   The breath is offensive, the respiration impeded, and the pulse high and sharp in *mad staggers*, whilst in *the sleepy* it is slow, heavy and full, without vibration.   When these latter symptoms continue a long time, the blood determines towards the head, and the pulse increases, if the animal be one in good condition.

The remedy is to bleed and purge.

Farm horses that live much in the straw yard, and work hard on bad hay, will sometimes stand still at once, as if struck motionless, in the midst of their work, which is a sure sign that some great leading function has been suspended for the moment by reason of great exertion.   The driver has nothing more to do in this case than to let the tired creature rest for the space of a minute or two, and then proceed in his work more leisurely.   Prevention is better than cure.

In all ordinary cases of staggers, simply opening the bowels will effect a cure nine times out of ten.

GRAZING.

Thin skinned horses that have been well kept and clothed should never be turned to grass above three months in the year, viz. from the beginning of *June* to the end of *August*.

Thick skinned horses have strong coats, which keep out the weather, and (if well fed) will lie abroad, and endure hard hunting all the year, better than stable horses. For, walking about to feed, prevents stiffness in their limbs; and treading in the grass keeps their hoofs moist and cool: but they should have a hovel to come to at night, or when it snows or rains.

Never purge a horse just taken from grass; it dissolves or loosens some tender fat or humours which fall into his legs or heels. But after six days you may bleed him once, under a quart; and at night give him the aniseed cordial, see page 57, which is a gentle opener.

NO COLD WATER WITH PHYSIC.

If you needs must purge your horse (for which I would have a good reason given) let him not touch cold water within or without, till the day after it has done working; but you cannot give him too much warm water. I wish he would drink enough, for the sake of dilution.

A PURGE.

Aloes, one ounce. Jalap, two or three drachms. Oil of cloves, ten drops: made into a ball with honey.

CAUTION AGAINST COLD WATER.

Some obstinate grooms will work it off with cold water; and tell you the sicker he is, the better the purge works. I deny it; for cold water checks the working of all physic, and causes gripings. Make that groom drink cold water gruel with his next pills, and that will convince him.

A purge may work the first day, but commonly does not till the second. I have known one lie two, nay three days in a horse, and work well off at last.

Sometimes it works by urine only, and then the purge steals off unobserved by his keeper ; upon which, he makes haste to give him a second, which (he says) is to carry off the first purge that has not worked with him. After giving the second, he takes him out of a warm stable, and trots him abroad (be the weather hot or cold) till he warms him and opens all the pores of his body to make the physic work. I do not think it possible for a horse with a purge or two in his belly to escape catching cold by such a method, and must impute great injuries to it ; for by such carelessness, and the want of better understanding, some horses lose an eye, others have irrecoverable lamenesses settled in their limbs, and many die. Then they tell you his liver was rotten, and his lungs (upon opening) all inflamed.

PURGE WITHIN DOORS.

How can any gentleman be satisfied for the loss of a good horse with such an ignorant account, so contrary to the rules of physic and even common sense? An understanding man, when he has given his horse a purge, will not stir him out of the stable till it has done working; for there is really no need of exercise during the operation, because every purge will carry itself off, if you keep him warm, and supply him with warm mashes, and as much warm water as he pleases to drink, and as often.

TO STOP VIOLENT PURGINGS.

When a purge works too long, or too strong upon him, which will weaken him too much, give him *an ounce of Venice molasses, in a pint of warm ale,* and repeat, if needful, to blunt the force of the aloes.

All the keepers at *Newmarket* bleed and purge the

running horses pretty often; and all the gentlemen in *England* agree with them in doing so. The reason given for it, is to carry off the humours which cause their legs to swell and grow stiff, and to clean them. The reason is good, because no horse is fit to run that is not clean; but bleeding and purging weakens both man and beast; besides the hazard of a horse's life in every purge (as I have demonstrated.) Would it not therefore be a good amendment to get quit of those superfluous humours another way, so as to prevent stiff and swelled legs without bleeding and purging? Would not a horse come into the field with better advantage, who, instead of bleeding and purging, only once a week takes a medicine that effectually cleans his body; keeps his legs from swelling and stiffness; mends his wind by opening his lungs, and preserves him in his full vigour? I am sure all this can be done with very little bleeding, and no purging; which I would willingly insert here, did it properly belong to this treatise, which (as I said) is intended only for the use and convenience of travellers.

IF A HORSE LOOKS ILL.—THE LAMPAS.— THE CURE.

If your horse (who once looked fat and sleek) is brought to you with a staring coat and hollow flank, open his mouth, look on the roof, and if the gums next his fore teeth are swelled higher than his teeth, it will hinder his feeding and make him fall off his flesh. Let a smith burn it down with a hot iron; that is a complete cure for the Lampas.

If that is not the cause, you should never cease enquiring till you have found it, for the horse cannot speak; and if the groom is in fault, he will not tell.

TAKE CARE OF YOUR HAY AND OATS.

If you suspect that the groom does not give him your allowance, it behooves you to take care, that you have thirty-six trusses in each load of hay, as well as eight bushels in every quarter of oats; and that they are not brewed; for there are some men that can turn oats into ale.

A CAUSE OF BROKEN WIND.

If a groom gallops his horse when he is full of water, he will tell you it is to warm the water in his belly; from hence often comes a broken wind. Make that fellow drink a full quart of small beer or water, and force him to run two or three hundred yards upon it: I believe it will cure him of that opinion. ✱

BAD GROOMS.—HOW TO DETECT THEIR TREATMENT OF YOUR HORSE

If a horse in his stall (when the groom comes towards him) shifts from side to side, and is afraid of every motion the man makes about him, it is a shrewd sign that the groom beats him in your absence; and a fellow that will beat a horse, will sell his provender.

ROWELS.

A rowel is a kind of issue made in a horse for inward strains, hard swellings, &c. But there is a wrong judged custom amongst farriers concerning them. If a horse is sick, they bleed him, right or wrong, give him a drench and put a rowel under his belly; without

7

enquiring of his master or keeper, what usage he has lately had which might occasion the illness. Rowels are absolutely necessary in some cases, but are absolutely unnecessary in others, and serve only to disfigure and torment a horse.

The rowel in the navel for grease is very wrong; because rowels in a horse that is greased, promote too great a discharge from the blood and animal spirits, which weakens him to a degree of irrecoverable poverty. I have put five rowels in a horse at one time, thinking (by them) to let the grease run off; but the more the rowels ran, the more he ran at the heels, till the texture of his blood was so broken, that I could not recover him. This convinced me it was the wrong way to cure the grease. I have heard it said amongst learned physicians, that too many setons or issues will draw a man into a consumption. In my opinion, rowels will do the same thing by a horse, as they are of like nature and effect.

GLANDERS AND FARCY.

The glanders is the opprobrium medicorum, for hitherto no attempts have succeeded in the cure of more than a few cases. By some peculiar anomaly in the constitution of the horse, although conclusive proofs are not wanting that this and farcy are modifications of one disease, and can each generate the other; yet the one is incurable, while the other is cured every day.

The marks of glanders are a discharge of purulent matter from ulcers situated in one or both nostrils, more often from the left than the right. This discharge soon becomes glairy, thick and white-of-egg-like: it afterwards shows bloody streaks, and is fœtid. The glands of the jaw of the affected side, called the kernels, swell from an absorption of the virus or poison, and as they exist or do not exist, or as they adhere to the bone or are detached from it, so some prognosis is vainly attempted by farriers, with regard to the disease; for in some few cases these glands are not at all affected, and in a great many they are not bound down, by the affection, to the jaw. As there are many diseases which excite a secretion of matter from the nose, and which is kept up a considerable time; so it is not always easy to detect glanders in its early stages. Strangles and violent colds keep up a discharge from the nostrils for weeks sometimes. In such cases, a criterion may be drawn from the existence of ulceration within the nose, whenever the disease has become confirmed. These glanderous chancres are to be seen on opening the nostril a little way up the cavity, sometimes immediately opposed to the opening of the nostril; but a solitary chancre should not determine the judgment. The health often continues good, and sometimes the condition also, until hectic takes place from absorption, and the lungs participate, when death soon closes the scene.

The following method is recommended as the best.

Dissolve one pound of glauber salts in warm water, set it in a bucket in his manger, and he will drink it; take half a gallon of blood from his neck vein; give a mash of two quarts of wheat bran scalded with sassafras tea, after which offer him lukewarm water, to drink, and do not suffer him to drink any other kind for that day; next morning take the same quantity of blood as before, give a mash as before, with the addition of half an ounce of saltpetre dissolved in it; let his food be wet, and of a weak kind—a run at grass after the first two days would be of service.

The *farcy* is a disease more easily cured than the

glanders, of which our daily experience convinces us; farcy, or farcin, attacks under distinct forms, one of which affects the lymphatics of the skin, and is called the bud or button farcy : the other is principally confined to the hind legs, which it affects by large indurations, attended with heat and tenderness. A mere dropsical accumulation of water in the legs sometimes receives the name of water farcy; but this has no connection whatever with the true disease in question : farcy is very contagious, and is gained from either the matter of farcy or from that of glanders.

Treatment of farcy.—The distended lymphatics or buds may often be traced to one sore, which was the originally inoculated part, and in these cases the destruction of this sore, and that of all the farcied buds, will frequently at once cure the disease, which is here purely local.   But when the disease has proceeded farther, the virus must be destroyed through the medium of the stomach ; although even in these cases, the cure is rendered more speedy and certain, destroying all the diseased buds, by caustic or by cautery. Perhaps no mode is better than the dividing them with a sharp firing iron ; or if deeper seated, by opening each with a lancet, and touching the inner surface with *lapis infernalis.* The various mineral acids may any of them be tried as internal remedies with confidence; never losing sight of the necessity of watching their effects narrowly, and as soon as any derangement of the health appears, to desist from their use; oxymuriate of quicksilver (corrosive sublimate) may be given in daily doses of fifteen grains; oxide of arsenic may also be given in similar doses. The subacetate of copper (verdigris) may also be tried, often with great advantage, in doses of a drachm daily. It remains to say, that whatever treatment is pursued will be rendered doubly efficacious

if green fodder be procured, and the horse be fed wholly
on it ; provided the bowels will bear such food ; but if
the medicines gripe, by being joined with green food,
add to the diet bean-meal. When green meat cannot
be procured, carrots usually can; and when they cannot,
still potatoes may be boiled, or the corn may be speared
or malted. As a proof of the beneficial effects of green
meat, a horse, so bad with farcy as to be entirely
despaired of, was drawn into a field of tares, and nothing
more was done to him, nor further notice taken of him,
although so ill as to be unable to rise from the ground
when drawn there. By the time he had eaten all the
tares within his reach, he was enabled to struggle to
more ; finally he rose to extend his search, and perfectly
recovered.

POLL EVIL.

An abscess near the poll of the horse, formed in the
sinews between the noll bone and the uppermost vertebræ
of the neck. If this malady originates in blows (as it
generally does) the best way will be to bathe the swelling as soon as it is perceived, frequently, with hot vinegar, and if the hair is fretted off with a kind of acrid
humour oozing through the skin, make use of two parts
of vinegar and one of wine. But if there be an itching,
with great heat and inflammation, the safest way is to
bleed freely, and apply a red oak poultice, which
method of proceeding, with the assistance of two or
three doses of purgative physic, will disperse the tumour
and arrest the disease. If, however, in spite of this pre-
caution, the swelling increases, and has all the signs of
containing matter, the only way left is to bring it to a
head as soon as possible, that it may be discharged either
by the tumour bursting of itself, or being opened with a

7 *

knife. In the latter case, however, great care should
be taken by the operator not to injure the tendinous liga-
ments which run along the neck, under the mane.
When matter lies on both sides, the opening must also
be on each side, that the ligament may remain undivided.
The following poultice should be used in bringing the
tumour to a head; marsh-mallows, corn-meal, hog's
lard, and oil of turpentine. If the matter flows in great
quantities, resembling melted glue, and is of an oily consistence, the cavity of the wound should be carefully
examined by the finger or probe, and further laid open
by the knife and dressed with spirits of turpentine, honey
and tincture of myrrh, until a light and thick-coloured
matter appears. Cleanse the sore well with a sponge
dipped in soap-suds; then take half an ounce of verdigris, four ounces oil of turpentine, two ounces blue stone
and half an ounce green copperas, which mix together
and hold over a fire until the mixture is as hot as a
horse can endure; then pour it into the abscess and
stitch it up. This must remain several days, without
any other application except bathing with spirits of wine.
When the matter becomes of a whitish colour and de-
creases in quantity, a cure is rapidly advancing.

RAT'S TAIL.

This is a malignant kind of disease in horses, resembling scratches. It proceeds sometimes from too
much rest, and the keeper's negligence in not rubbing
and dressing them well; also by reason of being highly
kept and not properly exercised. This disease makes
its appearance on the back sinews, and may be known
by the part being without hair, and from two or three
fingers' breadth below the ham to the very pastern.

joint. Sometimes the scabs are dry, at other times watery. The moist sort generally is cured by drying applications; and the dry hard sort mostly yields to strong mercurial ointment.

Coach horses of a large size, that have their legs loaded with flesh, hair, &c., are more frequently attacked by this than horses with legs of a different description; but they may easily be cured by paying attention to the following directions—in the first place, ride the horse pretty smartly till he is warm, which will make the veins swell; then bleed him freely in the fetlock veins on both sides. Next day wash the sores well with warm water, and clip away all the hair from about the affected parts, and apply this ointment: green copperas and verdigris, of each four ounces; of common honey, half a pound; well mixed together.

ANTICOR

Consists in an inflamed swelling of the breast near the heart, and the name is extended to any other swelling from this part back under the belly, even to the sheath, which also swells: in this event anticor is decidedly dropsical.

The cause of it is full feeding without sufficient exercise. Hard riding or driving, and subsequent exposure, or giving cold water to animals that are fleshy in the forehand, combined with a vitiated state of the blood, produce those extended swellings that partake somewhat of the nature of swelled limb in grease, and yet terminate in abscess when the case is a bad one.

The symptoms are an enlargement of the breast, that threatens suffocation. The animal appears stiff about the neck, looks dull and drooping, refuses his food, and trembles or shivers with the inflammation, which may be felt. The pulse is dull and uneven. If the disease owes its origin to dropsy, each pressure of the finger will remain pitted a few moments after the finger is withdrawn.

To repress the swelling, bleed copiously; give purgatives and clyster him; give bran mashes, and let the chill be taken off his water. Foment the throat and breast with bran mash or marshmallows, every four or five hours; and when these have reduced the symptoms, give an alterative ball of 2 drachms tartar emetic, and half an ounce Venice turpentine, mixed with liquorice powder enough to make the ball for one dose. Give one every eight-and-forty hours.

If the swelling depend upon dropsy, let a fleam or horse-lancet be struck into the skin at four or five places distant from each other, and in the lowest part of the swelling. From these punctures a watery discharge will take place, that relieves the patient hourly, and the issue of the matter is to be promoted by keeping open the sores with a seton, the tape being daily saturated in a mixture of 2 oz. spirits of wine, and 1 scruple corrosive sublimate. This will keep open the orifice until the offensive matter has run off, and is succeeded by the more healthy issue of thicker consistency and nearly white. On this appearance the seton is to be withdrawn, and the parts dressed with digestive ointment, the animal physicked once or twice with a moderate *purging ball* or six or seven drachms of aloes, and the cure will complete itself with the ordinary dressings.

THE STRANGLES.

This, as the name imports, is first indicated by a coughing and difficulty of swallowing, as if the animal would die of strangulation. It is a disorder of youth, (like our hooping-cough), is inherent to the nature of the animal, (as is our small-pox) once only, and its virulence may be abated by inoculation. It is sometimes attended with high fever; the appetite fails, the horse dwindles away very fast and wears a dejected look.

The symptoms are—a swelling commences between the upper part of the two jaw-bones, or a little lower down towards the chin, and directly under the tongue. A cough, and the discharge of a white thick matter, follow; with great heat, pain, and tension of the tumours, and of all the adjacent membranes, to such a degree that the animal can scarcely swallow. The eyes send forth a watery humour, and the lid is nearly closed: this is mostly the case when it happens that the two larger glands under the ear are affected also, which frequently happens.

This disorder is seldom fatal; but when this does occur, the animal dies of suffocation; he stands with his nose thrust out, the nostrils distended; the breathing is then exceedingly laborious and difficult, and accompanied by rattling in the throat.

For this last mentioned extreme case, no other remedy is found than making an opening in the windpipe, through which the animal may breathe.

On the contrary, the disorder being constitutional, that is to say, an effort of nature to relieve itself of noxious matters, the treatment is very simple. Horses that may be in good condition at the time of the attack, and withal highly feverish and full of corn, will only require opening medicine; whilst a brisk purgative might do harm by lessening the access of matter to the tumour. Give the following laxative ball:—Aloes and Castile soap, each 3 drachms; Ginger 1 scruple; mixed for one dose. If difficulty of swallowing is already perceivable, a laxative drench must be given instead, viz. Castor oil 6 oz, water gruel 1 qt, and salts 6 oz, mixed.

The essence of this disease consists in the formation and suppuration of the tumour under the jaw, and our principal aim should be to hasten it to a head, to do which it should be actively blistered. A blister not only secures the ripening of the tumour, but hastens it by many days. Do not be premature in using the lancet, but give time for the *whole matter* to collect; when this period arrives, the swelling will be soft and yielding—it should then be deeply and freely lanced. It is bad to let the swelling burst of itself, because a ragged ulcer is formed, very slow to health and difficult of treatment. If the incision is deep enough no second collection of matter will form. Suffer that already formed to ooze slowly out, without, however, any pressure of your fingers. It should be kept clean, and you should daily inject into the wound a small quantity of friar's balsam.

If after this there is much fever and an affection of the chest, bleeding should be resorted to; but in most cases bleeding will be unnecessary—not only so, but injurious,—because it will retard the suppuration of the tumour and increase debility. Nitre, tartar emetic, and cooling medicines should be administered; and he should have green food, such as fresh-cut grass or tares, if they are to be had, and bran mashes; if not to be had, such as is light and not difficult to digest. If the complaint lasts long and extreme debility is produced, malt mashes should be substituted for bran.

VIVES.

This disorder bears a near affinity to the strangles. The symptoms are swellings or kernels under the ear, that occasion manifest pain when touched; the animal coughs more than one which has the strangles, and a difficulty of swallowing soon is evident. Stiffness of the neck follows, and the horse makes frequent efforts to swallow the saliva, but is unable.

The cure of the vives that arises from a simple is very easy, but not so that which is connected with a general bad habit of the body. Oftentimes it happens that the vives depend upon glanders or farcy, and will only subside when the virulence of these is reduced.

Foment the part with warm water, and after it has been well dried, clothe the head so as to keep off the air. Much of the pain and tension of the tumour will be alleviated by this treatment, even, and a slight attack will be entirely removed by following it up with fomentations of marshmallows; or anoint the parts with ointment of marshmallows, and cover the head with clothing. A bread poultice affords relief, and bleeding in stubborn cases is often necessary, with purgatives. The body, in fact, should be *opened*, whether we bleed or no : always leave open the main road for such humours to escape by. This alone will carry off a recent attack, provided the head clothing be kept on at the same time, nature performing the remainder by absorption. Low diet, a plentiful supply of water gruel, and bran mashes, to which an ounce of nitre may be added daily, will reduce that thickened state of the blood which ever attends this species of tumour.

False vives, or imperfect ones, that are hard and insensible, sometimes cause a good deal of needless trouble. They neither come forward nor recede, do not seem to cause any particular pain, but still continue an *eye-sore* and give reason to apprehend disagreeable consequences; and always prevent an advantageous sale of an animal. Stimulating embrocations are well calculated for reducing these hard tumours, and the blistering liniment, made of cantharides and oil, never fails.

BARBS.

Barbs are excrescences or knots of superfluous flesh, found under the tongues of horses, and are to be easily discovered by drawing them to one side. The cure is to be effected by cutting them close off, and afterwards washing the part with salt and water or brandy, nor should the cure be postponed or neglected when a discovery has been made of the disease, for though it may appear as a trifling matter, it will hinder a horse from drinking, and if he does not drink freely, he cannot eat heartily, but will languish from day to day without any one perhaps taking any notice of it.

GIGGS UPON THE LIPS.

Giggs, otherwise called BLADDERS, or FLAPS ; are a disease in the mouth of a horse, consisting of small swellings or pustules with black heads, on the inside of his lips, under his great jaw teeth, which will sometimes increase to the size of a large walnut, at which advanced state they are so painful, that the horse will let his meat fall out of his mouth, or keep it there unchewed, sooner than attempt to eat it. These bladdders are generally produced from foul feeding, and are to be cured by opening them with a sharp knife, and thrusting out the kernels, or corruption, and afterwards washing the place with vinegar and salt, or with alum water. But if they should degenerate into the canker, it will be the best way to dress them two or three times with honey of roses, and spirits of vitriol, mixed in such proportions as to be pretty sharp of the latter ingredient.

RINGBONE.

A hard swelling on the lower part of a horse's pasterns, that generally reaches half round on the fore part, and derives its name from the resemblance it bears to a ring. It often arises from bruises, strains, &c., and, when it comes behind, which is sometimes the case, from the animal's being put frequently upon his haunches while too young, for in that attitude a horse throws the weight of his body as much (or more) upon his pasterns than upon his hocks.

When a ringbone appears distinctly round the pas-tern, and does not run down the coronet, so as to affect the coffin joint, it is easily cured; but if it takes its rise from some strain or affection of the joint itself, or if a callosity is formed under the round ligament that covers the joint, the cure is at best doubtful, and frequently im-practicable, as in this case it too frequently degenerates into a quittor, and forms an ulcer upon the hoof. Those ringbones that appear on colts, &c., will frequently go away of themselves, without any application at all, and when the substance remains, a blister or two will in gen-eral remove it, except, by being let alone too long, it has acquired a great degree of hardness and callosity, in which case it will perhaps require both blistering and firing.

To ensure the success of the last mentioned operation on ring bones, it should be performed with a much thin-ner instrument than what is commonly made use of for that purpose, and the lines or rases should be made at little more than a quarter of an inch distance, crossing them obliquely; and when this is done, a mild blister should be applied over the whole, and the horse turned out to grass.

FISTULA.

A kind of ulcer, which is long, narrow, and winding, and generally has a callous inside. The seat of a fistula is in the cellular membrane, and is known to be present when there is a small aperture or opening on the surface of the body, from which a sanious or other matter, either flows spontaneously, or may be pressed out; its depth and direction is discovered by introducing a probe, or if its directions are various, as is sometimes the case, warm water may be injected therein, which will show the course it takes, if that is near the skin, by elevating it; and if it is too deeply seated to be thus observed, the quantity of water thrown in will be a criterion whereby to judge of the size of the cavity. The probe will indeed discover whether or not the sinus runs upon a bone, or if the bone be carious, which water will not do. The various parts in which these ulcers are seated, and the different circumstances which attend them, constitute the chief difference betwixt one fistula and another. As to prognostics, the thicker the cellular membrane is, or the more strata, or layers of muscles one over another, the more mischievous a fistula will prove. While it is simple, and extends no farther than it can be wholly come at by a knife, it may be easily cured, but when it is situated in parts that render the use of the knife hazardous, or when it is complicated with a caries of the bone, the cure is often difficult if not impossible. When fistulas which are not yet become callous, are complicated with ulcers, the most expeditious relief is obtained by laying them open to the bottom, if it can be done without running any great risk, after which they are to be cleansed and healed as simple wounds. Another method of effecting a cure, is by pressing their bottoms towards their orifices by the help of a proper compress, which must be applied to its bottom after the ulcer is cleansed, and proper applications have been put into the fistula. Some practitioners reprobate all kind of injections, but when they lie so deep that their lower parts

cannot be cleansed by any other means, detergent injections must of course be used, such as a decoction of
birtwort mixed with honey, or with the simple tincture
of myrrh.   These, or something else of a like nature,
must be injected warm at every dressing, and retained
for a little time, at the same time compressing gently the
bottom and orifice of the fistula, that the peccant matter
may be the more effectually washed away; and this
method must be continued until the bottom of the fistula
begins to be conglutinated; then dress with some mild
digestive, to which is added a little of the balsam of Peru
or capivi.

Should this method fail of effecting a cure, the man-
ual operation must be attempted, but even this is not to
be depended on, unless you can make the incision to the
very bottom of the ulcer.   Nothing is better adapted to
perform this operation than the knife, but whatever
instrument is made use of, the skin and flesh that cover
the diseased part, must be divided to the bottom; for
when fistulous ulcers are laid thoroughly open, the corrupted matter is not only better discharged, but proper
medicines are more commodiously applied.   If, upon
making the incision, a large quantity of blood is discharged, you may fill the wound with dry lint, and
when the callosities are either pared away with the knife,
or wasted by the use of eschorate medicines, the cure
will be effected in the same manner as other simple
wounds.   As for the corrosive injections, which are recommended by some authors, they can be of no use
whatever.   Indeed, any person who is acquainted with
the manner in which such things operate on the body,
will be convinced, that instead of being serviceable, they
must aggravate the disease, by making the callosity and
hardness of the sides greater and more difficult to be
removed.

THE YELLOWS OR JAUNDICE.

A distemper with which horses are frequently affected. It is known by a dusky yellowness of the eyes; the inside of the mouth and lips, the tongue, and the bars of the roof of the mouth looking yellowish at the same time. The horse is dull and droops his head; his excrements are hard and dry and of a pale yellow, or pale green colour; he stales with pain and difficulty, and his urine is of a dark brownish colour, and leaves on the ground an appearance of blood.

Young horses and fat ones are easily cured.

Purge him; give him bran mashes, green food, and succulents, according to the season. Bleeding is seldom necessary or proper, which the state of the pulse will show.

STRING-HALT.

String-halt, in horses, is a sudden twitching or snatching up of the hind legs much higher than the other, to which imperfection the most spirited and mettlesome horses are unfortunately the most subject. It is generally brought on by sudden colds after hard riding or severe labour, particularly by washing a horse, while he is very hot, with cold water, a practice that cannot be sufficiently reprobated. It may likewise be occasioned by a blow or bruise near the hock.

The opinions of authors about the cure of this complaint are various; some recommend cutting a tendon which lies under the hinder vein of the thigh; others the use of liniments, ointments, fomentations, &c.; but in general the cure is difficult, and seldom effected.

RUNNING THRUSH.

Running Thrush, in horses, is an ulcerated or varicous state of the frog, attended with a discharge of acrid corrosive ichor, which sometimes quite destroys it.   This complaint is generally occasioned by inattention, and in its earliest stages is by no means hard to be cured.   In all cases it will be prudent, and even necessary, to pare away as much as possible of the diseased parts, and wash away any filth that may be lodged on the adjoining ones, with a lather of soft soap and water, after which the feet should be constantly stopped with cowdung, or something of a similar nature.   Should the complaint not give way to this treatment, there may be reason to apprehend that it is owing to a vitiated state of the fluids, in which case a few doses of alterative physic may be useful; but, perhaps, turning the horse out to grass for a month or two, if the season admits thereof, is by far the best method of attempting the cure.

CORNS.

Causes.—An entire series of disorders, as canker, sand-crack, corn, and founder, may be referred to the same original causes; namely, a heated or inflammatory state of the blood, which accident may concur to bring forward in one or other form, according to circumstances. Distortion and undue pressure on the *sensible sole* occasions that irritation which brings on inflammation of its edge, where the shuttle-bone, or *heel-bone*, presses down upon it at every step, and causes the utmost bending that the minute elasticity of the hoof allows of; but contraction of the heel, which accompanies hot, brittle, and inelastic hoof, prevents its bending duly and

8 *

truly, and lateral pressure upon the quarter follows. The sole being thus unduly pent up, the circulation is obstructed in its passage to and from the cavity of the coffin-bone, and a deposit of blood, which soon becomes offensive matter, is the consequence. Bad shoeing, whereby the heels are pinched, also when the ragged hoof is left, which may have contained particles of sand, will cause irritation, and end in *corn*, or *figg*.

Symptoms.—The mischief thus commenced within, shows itself between the bar and the crust, or wall of the hoof, in a foxy or dirty-red tumour, with greatly increased heat. *Lameness*, in a degree proportioned to the badness of the corn, is usually the first symptom that directs our attention to the sole. *Figg* is but another name for the same kind of corn when situated close to the bar of the frog, a little farther back in the hollow of the sole. Pain, very acute on the touch; or, when the horse treads on a hard substance, he issues a moan, or grunt: it is that sound in which his *voice* is aptly likened to the *complaint* of the human sufferer.

Cure.—Although oftentimes very troublesome, returning again and again when the *farrier* apprehends he has cured it *radically*, yet no affection is easier of a *partial* remedy, or effected by more ordinary means. Deceived by the name, perhaps, resembling the hard excrescence called a corn on the human foot, they proceed at once to " pare the corn out to the quick, *till the blood starts ;*" but they heedlessly put on the same shoe upon the same thick heel and hard hoof which first brought about the malady, and the lameness returns. Let the heel of the shoe be cut off on the side that is afflicted, or if both sides have corns, a bar shoe is recommended as giving pressure to the frog. The heels are then to be rasped away free from any contact with the shoe ; if they are thick and hard, this will give them play—if thin and tender, they will thus be freed from pressure. The *thick heel* is most commonly affected, and should be softened by an extensive poultice that is to cover the whole foot, after the *corn* has been pared and treated with *butter of antimony.* *Tar* is then a very desirable application, or *Friar's balsam ;* and if inflammation is again discovered, poultice the foot once more. *Fire* is applied by some, but the hoof is permanently injured by the actual cautery ; and whatever good is achieved is thus counterbalanced by the evil. Vitriolic acid mixed, *carefully*, with tar, in the proportion of one-tenth of the former to nine-tenths of the latter, will promote the absorption upon which the cure depends.

But in some desperate bad cases the matter has already formed within, most offensively, and discharges at the coronet by means of that curious process of nature which affords the coronet the material for forming new horn to supply the wear and tear of the hoof. Upon paring away the horny sole, which now becomes necessary, the offensive matter will be found to have spread itself underneath the sensible sole, which will ooze forth and give immediate relief to the coronet. Let so much of the horny sole as lies loose from the sensible sole be pared away, and a dressing of tar, or of Friar's balsam, be applied as before directed ; and if inflammation is again discovered, apply a bread poultice; should the growth of horn be found too luxuriant, discontinue the tar.

Where it has been necessary to remove much of the corn, the horse should be suffered to remain in a loose . place, or be turned out to grass until the horn is regenerated.

A FEVER.—A CURE.

Would you know when a horse is in a fever ? There is a pulse a little above the knee, in the inside of his leg, which may be felt in thin-skinned horses, but the best and surest way, is to put your hand to his nostrils, and discover it by the heat of his breath.

Fever is a disease that frequently attacks horses, the symptoms of which are, extreme restlessness, the creature ranges from one end of the rack to the other, his flanks beat, his eyes are red and inflamed, his tongue parched and dry, his breath hot and strong, he loses his appetite, and nibbles at his hay, but without chewing it, and is frequently seen to smell at the ground. The whole body is hotter than common, though not parched, as in some other disorders; he dungs often, but little at a time, and that is generally hard and in little bits. When he stales it is frequently with difficulty, and his urine is high coloured; he appears thirsty, but drinks only a small quantity at a time, though often, and his pulse beats full and hard, and fifty or more strokes in the space of a minute. The first thing to be done when the disorder is clearly ascertained, is to bleed to the quantity of two quarts, if the horse is strong and in good condition, after which give him a pint of the following drink four times a day, or an ounce of nitre made into a ball with a little honey may be given twice or three times a day instead of the drink, if it should be better approved of, and washed down with three or four horns of gruel, or some other diluting liquor:

Take baum, sage, and chamomile flowers, of each an handful, liquorice root, sliced thin, half an ounce, salt prunel or nitre, three ounces; infuse the whole about an hour in two quarts of boiling water, then strain off the liquor, and squeeze into it the juice of two or three lemons, and sweeten it with a little honey.

As the principal ingredient to be depended on in this drink is the nitre, it might, perhaps, in some respects, be as well given in water alone; but as a horse's stomach is soon palled, and he requires medicines that are some-what palatable, the other things may in some respects have their share of utility. Some recommend for the same purpose, to dissolve two ounces of cream of tartar, and one of sal ammoniac in two quarts of water, which is afterwards to be mixed with a bucket of common water, and given the horse for his drink, adding a hand-ful of bran or barley-meal, to take off the unpleasant taste, and render it more palatable. The following drink is also good in fevers:

Take Russian pearl ashes, one ounce, distilled vine-gar a pint, spring water a quart, honey four ounces, and when mixed, give a pint three or four times a day.

This neutralized mixture, and the nitre mixture before prescribed, may be taken alternately; they are both effi-cacious medicines, and in some cases may, with propri-ety, be joined to the camphorated julap. While horses are taking these medicines, their diet should be scalded bran, given in small quantities at a time; and should they refuse that, let them have raw bran sprinkled with water, and a handful of picked hay may be put into the rack, which they will frequently eat, while they refuse every other species of food. Their water should not be much warmed, but should be given them often, and in small quantities. Their clothing must be light, as too much heat and weight on a horse that has a fever would be improper. If in a few days the horse that is thus treated begins to eat his bran, and pick a little hay, this method only need be pursued, and in a few days the danger will be over. But if he refuses to feed, and the other symptoms still continue the same, or rather in-crease, it will be necessary to take away more blood: after which, the drinks may be continued with the addi-tion of about three drachms of saffron, avoiding at present all hotter medicines: the following clyster may likewise be given, every day or oftener, if there should be occasion, particularly if his dung be hard and dry:

Take marshmallow leaves, two handfuls, half as many chamomile flowers, and fennel seed, an ounce; boil the ingredients in three quarts of water, till it comes to about two, then strain it off, and add four ounces of honey or treacle, and a pint of linseed oil.

Two quarts of water-gruel, or fat broth, with the treacle and oils may be substituted in the place of the above, to which a handful of salt may be added, and these sort of clysters are much more proper in such cases, than those which consist of strong cathartic ingredients. The following opening drink is sometimes very effectual, and may be given every other day, when the clyster should be omitted:

Take cream of tartar and glauber's salts, of each four ounces, dissolve them in barley-water or gruel: an ounce or two of the lenitive electuary, or a drachm of jalap in powder, may be added to quicken the operation, where the case is urgent.

The diet should be very regular, and no kind of corn should be given, but let scalded or raw bran sprinkled with water be the principal food, with now and then a little hay, which should be picked and given out of the hand, if the horse cannot lift his head to the rack, as is frequently the case. After he has been treated in this manner for about a week, and the fever begins to go off, he may have a cordial ball given him once or twice a day, with an infusion of liquorice root sweetened with honey, to which may be added (when he is troubled with tough phlegm, or a dry husky cough) a few ounces of salad oil, and syrup or oxymel of squills.

There is every reason to expect that a speedy recovery will be effected when the fever is found to abate, the mouth to be less parched, and the grating of the teeth but little heard; when the horse begins to eat, and lay himself down, when his skin feels kindly, and his eyes appear lively. But, on the other hand, if the appetite gets no better, or if worse, and the heat continues to increase, the case is dangerous. Sometimes there is a running at the nose, which is generally of a reddish or greenish dusky colour, and a clammy consistence, sticking to the hairs within the nostrils. Now, whenever this running becomes clear and watery it is a good sign, but if it continue thus tough and ill coloured, the horse at the same time sneezing frequently, his flesh continuing flabby, and he feeling hide bound, or if his weakness increases, and the joints swell, the kernels under the jaws feeling loose, though they are swelled, or if the tail is lifted up with a kind of convulsive quivering motion, you may conclude that death will soon step in to his relief.

Intermitting fevers will rarely admit of bleeding, at least the quantity of vital fluid taken away should not be great ; the best way of attempting the cure being to give an ounce of Peruvian bark in fine powder every fourth hour during the absence of the fever, and should that run off with a purging, a little diascordium, or other gentle astringent may be added to prevent that effect. In case of any other fever's coming to intermit regularly, it may be treated in the same manner as though it had been a regular intermittent from the beginning.

The low, or putrid kind of fever, seldom admits of bleeding ; but if from any symptoms that appear at the time, it should be thought necessary, the utmost caution and circumspection should be used, as the symptoms which seem to call for this evacuation will soon subside, from the nature of the disease itself. However, if the horse is young and vigorous, and his vessels appear filled with rich dense blood, a little may with propriety be taken away in the beginning of the disease.

Whether or not it is thought necessary to take away blood in the beginning of epidemical and contagious fevers, the following cordial saline mixture should be given as soon as the disorder manifests itself to be of that description :

Take mindererus's spirit four ounces, camphorated julap a pint, Virginian snake-root, half an ounce, and saffron reduced small, three drachms, to which add a pint of weak cinnamon water, and give half of it night and morning.

If, notwithstanding the use of this medicine, his complaint appears to gain ground, let the following cordial ball be added to each dose of the mixture :

Take bark finely powdered, an ounce, Virginian snake-root half an ounce, camphor a drachm, and with a sufficient quantity of honey make a ball.

If the horse is costive, laxative clysters should now and then be given, or in their stead some gentle purges, to clear the bowels from any putrid matter that might lodge there and feed the disease; but if a purging comes on, and seems to weaken him much, it must be checked with opiates, and gentle astringents; though, if it is moderate, it may as well be let alone, such gentle evacuations being frequently efforts of nature to carry off the disease. Many more prescriptions for fevers might have been selected from various authors, for the cure of fevers, but the above seem to be the best adapted for the purpose: where the methods here recommended fail, or where any other ingredient is thought necessary, the judicious practitioner will find a variety of drugs described in the course of the work, and their natures and properties explained, so that he may vary his medicines in such a manner as circumstances may require, and indeed every practitioner that pays a proper regard to the subject, will find such a method of proceeding frequently necessary : nothing being a more positive proof of ignorance and stupidity, than to suppose the same disorder will, in different constitutions, always submit to the same mode of treatment.

The following fever powders are used: 1. Two drachms of tartar emetic and five drachms of nitre.— 2. Two drachms of antimonial powder, and four drachms each of cream of tartar and nitre.

The following fever drink can be recommended : one oz. spirits of nitre, six oz. minderus spirit, and four oz. of water.

SWELLED NECK.—CURE.

If a farrier, in bleeding, miss the vein, do not let him strike his fleam a second time into the same place ; because it sometimes makes the neck swell, and proves troublesome to cure : and as the extravasated blood infallibly makes the neck swell, and the jugular vein rot quite away from the orifice up to the jaw-bone, and downward almost to the shoulder, (which may prove the loss of your horse ;) he should take care, in the pinning, that he leaves not a drop of blood between the flesh and the skin.

Note.—The nearer the throat you bleed him, the better. The vein is not so apt to swell into a knot, as if bled lower.

The turnip poultice makes the best cure; but if the neck should happen to be extremely bad and a tumour should form, when you feel matter fluctuate under your finger, it is best to open it and give a free discharge, and dress it with the horse-ointment, keeping the neck elevated.

A horse after bleeding should not eat hay for half a day, lest the motion of the muscles should bring on an inflammation and swelling.

9

DOCKING.

1. seldom happens that we dock a horse upon a journey, but permit me to give a caution on that subject here. In docking a horse, never put under his tail the knife or instrument which is to cut it off; because then you must strike the tail, which will bruise it, and it will be apt to mortify; but lay his tail next the block, and (at one blow) drive the knife through a joint, if possible; stand prepared with a hot iron to sear the end of the dock and stop the bleeding.

FLIES—HOW TO KEEP THEM OFF.

Rub your horse every morning with walnut leaves: it is certain to secure them from flies and other insects.

I have now mentioned most of the common accidents, and have taken care, that under some of those heads, you may find a great deal of help by the analogy they have to one another: and having added more than is necessary on a journey, I beg leave to end.

There is no drug or composition put in here, but what is very cheap, and may be had almost in every country village you travel through; so I hope I have left no difficulty on any body. But if I should be condemned by some, for presuming to leave the beaten paths of all the well known authors that wrote before me, how could I answer to others, had I neglected an improvement which may turn to the general good of man and beast?

I have read all I could find, and have tried their receipts with great attention and expense; and can say, it was experience alone that led me into the knowledge of contracting overgrown receipts, hastening cures, and moderating costs.

www.ingramcontent.com/pod-product-compliance
Lightning Source LLC
Chambersburg PA
CBHW032202010726
47493CB00008BA/2789